SEA-SPELL AND MOOR-MAGIC

SEA-SPELL

AND
MOOR-MAGIC
Tales of the Western Isles

by SORCHE NIC LEODHAS

illustrated by VERA BOCK

Holt, Rinehart and Winston

NEW YORK   CHICAGO   SAN FRANCISCO

For my semi-secretary
Jill Digby
moran taing

The pictures are for L. T.

Contents

Each of the stories in this book came from a different island in the Scottish Hebrides, or Western Islands. The island from which each story came is listed below.

Contents

Introduction

In the tales that come out of the Hebrides there is a preoccupation with the sea, not strange in an island people who lived out their days within sight and sound of it, and who knew it intimately in all its seasons: the raging gales and cruel breakers of its winters; the freshening winds and rains and the gentler tides of its spring; the sweet breezes and calm days, so often broken by the sudden and terrible thunderstorms of its summer; the gusty surges and blows of its autumn with their promise of winter to come. Beneath the conscious thoughts of every islander as he pursued the affairs of his everyday life lay always his awareness of the eternal presence of the sea. It is not strange, then, to discover that the sea, in some fashion, appears in almost every tale that is told in the Western Isles.

The sea plays a part in seven out of the ten stories in *Sea-Spell and Moor-Magic*.

In "The Son of the Baker of Barra," Ian Beg, seeking his castle, travels to the great empty green sea at the end of his world, and after he has found and lost his castle, to retrieve it he sails over the western sea to the Island of the Kingdom of the Rats.

In "The Ceabharnach" (pronounced kev-ur-nahk), the hero crosses the sea to Erin by stepping on apples which he tosses into the waters before him to make steppingstones, and when he makes his return journey he steals a corrach from the Irish shore and rows home. (There may be the remnant of an old myth in this tale, because *ceabharnach* means a tippler, or a happily intoxicated person, but it also means a mischievous breeze of wind.)

In "The Three Teeth of the King," the king's sons and the hero make a long voyage to an island ringed about with fire. This fire-girt island appears in a number of Hebridean stories and folklorists say that it was probably Iceland with its many volcanoes. Men from the Islands who saw it on their voyages came back to tell of its wonders, and their adventures were woven into many of the old folk tales. When one considers how small these early craft were, and how frail—many of them were only corrachs made of hides stretched over a framework of wood, such as are still used here and there by fishermen in the Isles to this day—one marvels that they dared to venture so far. It is a miracle that any of them lived to return home to tell about it.

In "The Water-Bull of Benbecula," the sea provides a fairy creature, the *Each-uisge* or Water-horse. All the supernatural beings of the sea (in which the island people believed even down to fairly modern times) were given the blame for otherwise inexplicable accidents in which persons lost their lives by drowning, in quick-sands, by falls from sea cliffs, or from boats which unaccountably capsized, and the like. The blame was always laid upon some water demon or other who had taken the traveler unaware.

"The Sea Captain," of course, is a sea story, pure and simple, and the strange island of the tale is the one known to the Scottish islanders as Eilean-h-oige, and to the Irish as Tir-nan-Og, and to both Scots and Irish occasionally as I-Brasil. In both languages the name has the same meaning, the Island of Youth. Sometimes it is known also as the Blessed Isle, and through the ages men have supposed it to be the final retreat of great heroes and holy men. It is a peculiar thing that there is no record of the death of Fionn, or Fingal, in any of the songs or stories told about him. If he is near to death in one tale he always appears fighting with might and main or sagely taking command in a later one. The ancient belief is that Fionn retired with the remnant of his trusty band who survived battle, and sailed to Eilean-h-oige, where everything is fair and lovely, where winter never comes and no one ever dies, and there he dwells to this day. Through the ages men have spoken of seeing this strange island, and seafarers have written much about it, but they never were able to sail close enough to it to put their ships in by the pier. Fog, or storm, or the falling of night always kept them from their goal. As late as 1930 some fishermen from Tiree, driven westward off their course by a storm, came back home to tell of seeing through the mists to the west the shadowy shapes of towers and houses and trees on what seemed to be a great island far across the sea. Unfortunately, the winds changed and they were blown eastward again, and soon the island was lost to their sight.

In "The White Sword of Light," when the prince loses the game to the brown, curly-furred giantess, the forfeit he must pay is to fetch the White Sword of Light, the famous *Claidheamh-geal-solus,* which is spoken of in many Gaelic tales. He sails from his own land (which may have been Islay) to the west coast of Jura, where he outwits the giantess and secures the sword. If you go to Jura today, they will show you there the *sgriob-nan-cailleach* (the furrow of the old woman). There are two deep ravines from the top of the hill down to the sea with two lines of great boulders at the end, and folk will tell you that these are the furrows dug by the heels of the giantess as she tried to save herself from sliding into the sea.

Although one cannot properly call "The Bauchan in the Family" a sea story, as the only sea voyage in it (when the MacLeods and the MacDonalds, and young MacIntosh and his wife, emigrate to America), is little more than mentioned, still the story has always given me a strong feeling of island life, and the battle of the islanders against the weather, which comes from the sea, and the isolation of their bit of land in the midst of the waters, gives it at least a toe hold on the sea-story class.

There are many more *gruagachs,* or giants, in the

tales from the Western Isles than there are in the lore of mainland Scotland. Both giants and giantesses are commonly known as gruagachs, and although the feminine form, denoting a giant woman, is *bean-gruagach,* it is seldom used. The reason for the preponderance of giant tales in the islands lies far back in Scottish history. Gruagach is quite probably a corruption of the word *druidhe,* the Gaelic name for the Druid priests and priestesses, who were, according to the ancient religious practice, chosen because of unusual intelligence, great stature and beauty of form, and reared to become leaders of the common people. The druidhe were believed to have great gifts of divination and magic, and it is held that many of them were of Scandinavian origin, so that they really were tall enough and broad enough to seem like giants to the smaller Scottish men and women. When the advance of the Christian missionaries drove the Druids from the mainland, many of them fled to the Islands and established strongholds there. Because of their location and their geographical formation, the Islands were natural fortifications, from which the Druids were with difficulty dislodged. So the tales of the gruagachs, are most likely the stories which the ancient island dwellers handed down, telling about the days when they were the terrified subjects of the Druids. As the stories were told and retold through generations, the tall, strong Druids became giants, and their magic gifts, which to begin with were, no doubt, partly an ability to make the people believe in those gifts, and partly a superior education and intelligence, became in truth the sorcery, the enchantments, and the spells of the tales as we know them now.

All the folk tales of the Hebrides, those misty western islands of the Scottish Highlands, have something of the quality of the Gaelic language in which they were so long told. They seem to have borrowed some of the rough sweetness of the wind that blows across the *machair*, bearing with it the honeyed scent of heather and wild thyme.

None of the island stories have distinct parallels in the traditional lore of other countries. There are a few incidents which resemble those in folklore of other lands, but these resemblances are slight and infrequent, and the stories, as a whole, have a character exclusively their own.

The ten tales in *Sea-Spell and Moor-Magic* come from the islands of Barra, Skye, Arran, Islay, Lewis, Mull, Benbecula, Jura, and Muck, and there is one of them which is attributed to no island but which tells about the mythical Island of Youth, Eilean-h-oige.

SEA-SPELL AND MOOR-MAGIC

The Son of the Baker of Barra

ONCE a baker of Barra had a son and one son only, and the son's name was Ian Beg. There was nothing amiss with the lad at all, except that he was so goodhearted that he'd give the coat off his back to anyone who wanted it, and follow it with his shirt if that was asked for too.

One day the baker of Barra made a very fine cake and told his son to take it up to the castle so that the king's daughter could have it for her supper.

"That I'll do, and gladly," said Ian Beg. "Give me the cake, then, and let me be on my way." So the baker laid the cake in a clean white cloth, and gave it into his son's hands.

It was a fair way to go to the castle, but the lad walked along briskly, carrying the cake by the corners of the cloth gathered into his hand. The road ran along by the burn, and then it ran along through the glen, and then it took a turn into a wood that stood in the way. There unders the trees Ian Beg met three old gray cailleachs, and he gave them *"Fáilte"* and bade them leave him go by. But the three old women stood in his way and would not let him pass.

"Fáilte, Ian, son of the baker of Barra," they said. "What is it that you have in the napkin, that you carry it with such care?"

" 'Tis a cake my father made for the daughter of the king," Ian answered proudly. "And 'tis myself that is taking it to her, that she may have it for her supper the night."

"For the king's daughter, do you say!" said the first old gray cailleach.

"Such a cake would be a wonder to see!" the second one said.

"Could you not open the napkin a wee bit and let us just have the smidgen of a look at it?" the third one begged.

Well, a bit of a look could do no harm, so Ian opened the napkin and showed them the cake. When he thought they had admired it long enough, he got ready to gather up the cloth about it so that he could be on his way again. But the three old cailleachs would not let him.

"Not more than two or three times in my life have I tasted such a cake," said the first one.

"Not more than once in my life have I done the same," sighed the second one.

And then the third one said, "Och, I have ne'er once, in all the days of my life, put so much as a crumb of such a cake in my mouth!"

Then, as if the thought struck them all at the one time, they cried out, "Och, Ian Beg, *mo graidh,* will ye not let us have a wee crumb to taste of the cake?"

Well, Ian being so goodhearted, although he wanted to say no, he could not do it. So he held the cake up on his hand, and told them they might each pinch off a wee crumb of it, but to make sure to take it where it wouldn't show.

And so they did. They savored the wee bit of a crumb with delight and Ian, pleased with their pleasure, forgot where his duty lay.

"Och, now, have a wee bit more," he pressed them kindly. " 'Twill ne'er be missed!" And to encourage them, he took a taste of the cake himself. Then one crumb followed another, and all of a sudden Ian Beg discovered the cloth was empty except for a few last crumbs. Among them all they'd finished the cake.

"Och, ochone," Ian Beg lamented. "Now the king's daughter will have no cake for her supper, and my father will flay the skin off my back when I go home."

"Och, nay, Ian Beg!" the first old cailleach told him. "Do you think so poorly of us to think we'd let you go home to face your father's wrath, and the three of us doing naught to save you?"

Then she took the cloth from his hand and folded it

carefully to keep the crumbs inside. The three old creatures passed it from one to another until it came back to the hands of the first one again. She put it into the hands of Ian Beg. "Carry the napkin home to your father," she bade him. "Tell him to shake it out over the table and I'll warrant he'll be leaving the skin of your back alone. That will pay you for what I had of the cake. As for my sisters, they will pay for their share some time when you're needing it more than now." And, as Ian Beg started off home, she called after him, "Tell your father to bake another cake for you to take to the king's daughter in the morn."

Ian Beg, being a biddable lad, did as he was told. When he got home his father asked him, "Were they liking the cake at the castle?" for he was eager to keep the castle trade.

"They were not!" said Ian Beg. "And how would they be liking it, the way they never got it?" he asked.

"Ne'er got it?" said the baker. "And why did they not?"

"Och, on the road through the wood I met three old gray cailleachs who begged so prettily for a taste of the cake that I let them have it." said Ian Beg. "And then they ate it all up."

"You let them have it!" roared the baker, reaching for his great wooden paddle that he put the loaves into the oven with. "Och, I'll be letting you have a bit of something too, my fine lad!"

"Not so fast," cried Ian Beg, skipping nimbly out of the way of the paddle. "Here's the cloth the cake was in,

6.

and they bade me tell you to shake the cloth out over the table, and you'd be willing to leave me be."

The baker grumbled, but he set the batter paddle aside. Taking the cloth in his hands he went over to the table, where he unfolded it and shook it out above the table top.

"Och! Crumbs!" he said, looking at them with disgust. "Losh! Have we not crumbs enough in our bakehouse now?" But before he had finished speaking every crumb had turned into a shining golden coin. "Look ye now, lad!" the baker cried joyfully. "Well paid am I for the cake, and no mistake. And a very good thing it was for you to let the old ones have the cake, for I'm thinking that they belong to the People of Peace, the fairy folk, themselves."

"I'd not be knowing about that," said Ian Beg. "They looked to me like any old cailleachs you might be meeting. But they said to tell you to bake another cake for me to take to the king's daughter in the morn."

As Ian Beg said, so it was done, and the next day Ian went off again with a cake for the king's daughter happed in a fresh white cloth which he carried with the four corners of it gathered into his hand. He went along by the burn, and then he went along through the glen, and into the wood and out of it again. This day he did not see the three old gray cailleachs at all, but when he came out of the wood and took the high road, he saw a great sluagh of gentlefolk all on their way to the castle like himself. Some rode by on horseback and some rolled by in carriages, but he was the only one with naught but his own legs to carry him there. So he strode along in the dust of their passing, and soon he found himself trudging along behind them all. When he got to the castle he asked the man who guarded the door what was the occasion that had brought so many of the gentry there that day.

" 'Tis the birthday of the daughter of the king," said the man. "And now that she is of an age to wed, she has given out the word that she will have for a husband the man who brings her the gift she likes the best."

" 'Tis nothing to me," said Ian Beg. "I am not in the running, for all I've brought is the cake that my father, the baker of Barra, made this morn for the supper of the daughter of the king."

So the man passed Ian Beg through the door, and Ian went into the castle hall with his cake.

The king sat in his chair of state at a long table, which was placed at one end of the hall. Beside him sat his daughter, ready to choose the gift that she preferred above all the rest. One by one, the gentlemen came up to the table and set their gifts upon it for her to see. Some of the gentles were very young, and some were very old, and the others were somewhere in between, but the lot of them all had the same proud and haughty look that showed they thought very well of themselves.

The richness of their gifts was beyond imagination, and soon the top of the table glimmered and glittered and shone with the gold and the silks and the precious stones that covered it from end to end. The king's daughter sat and looked down at the brave show with

8 .

as little interest as if all these rich things were no more than pebbles and shells and driftwood, such as a bairn might find along the shore.

When the last gift had been laid on the table, and the suitors had drawn off to the side to wait until the choice was made, Ian Beg walked up, and pushing some of the gifts aside to make room for it, he set his cake down on the table in front of the daughter of the king.

" 'Tis no gift at all that I'm bringing you," he told her. "Naught but a cake that my father, the baker of Barra, made for your supper this night."

The king's daughter looked at the cake and then she looked at the lad who had brought it. Her eyes began to smile but as yet her lips did not. "*Moran taing!* Thank you!" she said gravely. "Thank you, son of the baker of Barra, for the cake. It will come in handy, this being my birthday, and us without a crumb of cake in the house before you came."

Her eyes saw more than the cake, although that was well worth seeing. What she saw, forbye, was that the lad was tall and well-built, a big, handsome, yellow-haired laddie, and under the dust that had gathered upon him, stirred up by the wheels of the carriages and by the horses' feet, his face was bonnie and good-humored, and she could tell that he was honest, too. But she asked him to stand to the side, for the moment, while she settled in her mind which of the gifts on the table she'd choose.

She looked the gifts over again, and then she looked at the suitors, and the more she saw of the latter the less she liked them. Slowly she rose from her chair beside the king, her father. The time had come for her to make her decision known. And so she did.

In a clear voice she said, "Jewels galore I have and more I need not. Silks I have in abundance—so many that I shall never wear them all. I am no longer a bairn so I have no use for your golden toys and trinkets. The gift I like best is the cake that was brought to me by the son of the baker of Barra, and he's the one I shall wed!"

Ian Beg thought that his ears belied him, but the king's daughter looked at him, and her lips were smiling now, as well as her eyes.

"Will you have me then, son of the baker of Barra?" she asked him.

Ian's heart leaped within him, for joy, and he answered. "Och, I don't mind if I do!"

Then there was a great to-do in the castle when the suitors understood that the king's daughter had passed them and their gifts by for a dusty baker's lad and a cake. They all seized their gifts in a great huff and went home. So there was the cake, sitting alone upon the table, with the king and his daughter behind it, and Ian Beg before.

"Well, my dear," said the king to his daughter, "I have naught to say against the baker of Barra. A very good baker he is, to be sure. And his son, no doubt, is a very fine lad. And this cake well may be, and probably is, the very best of cakes. But after all, a cake is a cake, and a husband is a husband. A cake is soon eaten and forgotten, and other cakes take its place. But a husband you must keep until the end of your days. Why not let the son of the baker of Barra go home to his father who will bake you a cake every day if you like?"

"Nay!" said his daughter. "My choice is made. I'll bide by it, come what may."

Och, this will not do at all! the king thought to himself. The world would ne'er stop laughing, should I let my daughter wed with a baker's son. He knew he'd never be able to argue his daughter out of it, for she was terribly set in her mind, and what she said she'd do, she intended to do. He sat looking at the pair of them, then he suddenly had what seemed to him a very good thought.

"Och, well," said the king to his daughter, "if you're of a mind to have the lad for a husband, I'll have naught to say against it. But you being my daughter, and my lone bairn, you'll understand I have your welfare at heart. No home have you e'er had in your life but in a castle, with all that was in it exactly as a king's daughter should have it. I have my doubts that you could be happy otherwise. You may wed the son of the baker of Barra with my blessing when he can give you a castle as good as this one, with everything in it the way you've always had it, forbye. Now I've had my say, and 'tis all I'll say."

The king's daughter looked sadly at Ian Beg, but Ian Beg gave her a great smile. "A man can but try," he told her. "Will you wait for me till I come back again?" he asked.

"Aye!" replied the king's daughter. "I'll wait."

Then Ian Beg went home and told his father what the king had said.

"Now, bake me some bannocks to eat on the road, and give me your blessing," said Ian Beg. "And I'll be off. The world will be my pillow and the sky will be my coverlet, and I'll find a castle for the king's daughter to live in or I'll not come back at all."

Ian Beg's father gave him a bundle of bannocks and his blessing and wished him Godspeed, and off Ian went on his journey. But though he traveled the length of the land, up and down and back and forth for many a weary mile, and saw many a strange sight upon the way, he could not find a castle for himself. At last he came to the end of the world, and there was no place farther for him to go, for there was nothing before him but the great empty green sea with the gray sky beyond it.

"Truagh mo charadh! How heavy my sorrow!" said Ian Beg, and he stood and stared hopelessly at the sea. Then his eye caught a glimpse of a house that stood beyond on the shore, and as the night was drawing in and he was weary, he thought he would go there and ask for shelter until the day's dawn. So up to the house he went, and the door was open, so he went in. There were three seated there at a table, and he saw in the blink of an eye that it was the three old gray cailleachs whom he had met in the wood. They looked up at him as he came in and cried out a greeting.

"Fáilte! Welcome, Ian Beg," said the first one.

"Mile fáilte! A thousand welcomes!" the second one said.

"Ceud mile fáilte! A hundred thousand welcomes!"

said the third. "Now that you're here, you must have a bite to eat with us."

So Ian Beg drew up a stool and sat down to the table. Then the old women discovered that he ate little, but sat leaning his head upon his hand, so they asked him how he came to be so sad. Soon they had coaxed all of Ian's troubles out of him, and himself was telling them everything that had happened to him since he last saw them in the wood.

"I've been up and down and back and forth through all the weary world, and there's not a castle that has not an owner to it already," Ian said.

"Och, I'd not say that," said the first old cailleach.

" 'Tis not impossible to find a castle," the second one said.

" 'Tis not, to be sure," said the third one. "Only you must choose the proper place to look."

"I'll give you a wee bit of something to help you," said the second old gray cailleach, and she took out of her sleeve a small black iron box. The three old women passed it about among them from one to another until it came into the hands of the second one again.

"I've not forgotten your kindness in sharing the cake with us," said she, as she put the wee box in his hands. "This will pay for what I had of it, but be careful to keep it always with you, for it is a box that can do you good or harm!"

Ian Beg thanked her, and took the box and dropped it into his pouch, but indeed, he could not see how such a wee box could help him, so he soon forgot about it.

But telling the old sisters about his troubles so relieved him that he felt as if a great load of grief had slipped off his back, and he slept very well that night.

In the morning they woke Ian Beg early and started him off upon his way home, bidding him to be of good heart for he'd be finding his castle very soon. So back he went through the world, up hill and down and over moor and mountain, and on the third day he came to a burn in flood and the water was too deep for crossing, so he sat down to rest a bit and cool his feet in the stream before seeking a better place to get across. While he was sitting there a hunger came on him, for all that day he had not passed so much as a shepherd's bothan where he could beg a bite to eat. As he felt around in his sporran to find if a bit of bannock remained there, his fingers came upon the box that the second gray sister had given him, so he took it out. Och, what was the good of a wee iron box, and what would be in it, forbye?

So he opened the box.

Out jumped three spry lads, crying out *"Easgadh!* Easgadh! Ready! Ready, Master Baker's Son!" and bowing low before Ian Beg, they asked politely, "What will you have us do for you?"

When Ian Beg got over his surprise, he told them to bring him food at once. Soon they brought him his dinner on a great silver tray, and waited upon him while he ate. When he had finished he told them that he needed nothing more, so into the box they popped. Ian shut the lid down upon them and put the box into his pouch again. "Och," said he, "if these creatures can bring me a dinner so easily, happen they can help me to a castle, too." Then off he went on his journey again, lighthearted and fast-footed, and within a few days, reached home.

The baker of Barra was happy to have his son back again. As for the castle, the baker was of the opinion that Ian was well enough off without it, and as for the king's daughter, who ever heard of one of those who wedded a baker's son?

Ian said naught one way or the other to all his father told him. He said not a word about the wee iron box either, but ate his supper and went early to bed.

While the moon was yet high and the night dark and still, Ian rose from his bed and got into his clothes. Out of the house he went, and down the road, along by the burn and through the glen, until he came to the wood. There he took out the wee box and opened it, and at once the three spry lads leaped out, crying "Easgadh! Easgadh! Master Son of the Baker! What will you have us do for you?"

"Build me a fine castle here, with the wood to be a park about it, and the castle to be bigger than the king's own and better. Make everything in it finer than anything in the king's house, and put a great stable behind it, and in the stable a gold coach with four white horses to draw it for me to go to the king's castle in, in the morn. And look to it that there be plenty of servants, both indoors and out, that the king's daughter and myself may be well served."

Long before cock's crow that morn all was done, exactly as Ian had commanded. The three spry lads were back in their box, and the box safely in Ian's pouch again.

When the sun was high in the sky that morn, Ian Beg dressed in his best and rode up to the king's castle in his gold coach drawn by four white horses with gold plumes on their heads. There was a fine coachman to drive the horses, with four footmen behind, and a postilion riding before. The king looked out the window and wondered who this grand laird was that came riding so fine. His daughter came and looked over his shoulder, and then she laughed aloud.

"Och, what way would your eyes be telling you 'tis a laird at all?" she asked. "Is it not plain to be seen that 'tis Ian Beg, come back to make me his bride?"

The king was terribly vexed. "Och, well," he grumbled, "happen the lad has got hold of a coach and four horses, but that does not mean he'll be having the castle, too."

"Aye, but he will!" the king's daughter said.

After the king saw Ian's castle, he could say no more against the wedding of his daughter to the baker's son. Had not the lad got a castle even bigger and better than his own? So the wedding was set for a week come Sunday, and the king's daughter hurried off to see to her wedding gown, while Ian Beg took his gold coach back to his castle and left it there. Then he walked home to his father's house and there wasn't a man in Barra that day could match him for happiness.

He was late getting to bed that night, because he had so much to tell his father, and it took time to make the baker understand that his baking days were over, and that he should sell his bakehouse and live at ease for the rest of his days. It wasn't until he was getting ready for bed that Ian discovered that his wee iron box was not in his pouch.

"Och, woe!" he said, yawning. "I've laid it down somewhere up at the castle, no doubt. Well, I'm too tired to go fetch it now. I'll rise early and go for it, in the morn." Half asleep, he tumbled into bed.

When the king came home from having a look at Ian Beg's castle, he sat and chewed his fingers with rage. There was some trick or other about the way Ian Beg's castle had appeared, but what it was he couldn't think. At least, he decided, he could go see the spae-wife and see what she could tell him. She had the name for having all sorts of uncanny wisdom, and folk called her a witch. Maybe she could tell him what to do.

So down the stairs he stomped, and out the back door of the castle and kept on going until he came to the spae-wife's cottage at the end of the hen run. The spae-wife cast her spells for him and then she said. "It has all been done with the help of a magic box that the People of Peace have given the baker's son. As long as he carried it with him there was nothing you could do about it, but by mischance he has mislaid it this night. You will find it where it has slipped down behind the cushions of his gold coach. My advice to you is to take your daughter at once to the castle, and when you have found the box tell those who come out of it when you open it to take the castle, yourself, and your daughter to some distant place where the son of the baker will not be able to find you."

"Well and good," said the king. "But where would such a place be?"

"The Island of the Kingdom of the Rats would be the best place," the spae-wife said. "I doubt he'll e'er have heard tell of it. You should be safe there."

The king did as the spae-wife told him. He went back to his castle and roused his daughter from her bed, and made her go to Ian's castle with him that very night. Long before Ian Beg woke in the morning the three spry lads from the wee black iron box had obeyed the king's command and carried the king and the king's daughter and the castle of Ian Beg to the Island of the Kingdom of the Rats far away over the sea, and set them all down there.

When Ian Beg went up the road to his castle in the morning his heart was blithe and gay, but when he got to the wood, it sank like a weight of lead. There was no sign of a castle among the trees, and all that was left was the bare empty space where it had stood.

Ian rushed up to the king's castle to tell the king's daughter that his castle was gone, but neither the king nor his daughter were at home, the servants said. All that they could say was that the king had taken his daughter and gone away with her in the night, and where he had taken her they would not be able to say, for they had not been told. So Ian Beg went back to the wood and sat down by the road, not knowing what else to do. While he was sitting there, along the road the three old cailleachs came, and stopped before him.

"Och, Ian Beg, *mo graidh*! What is the trouble now?" they said.

Ian Beg looked up at them and answered. "Och, my castle is gone, and the king's daughter, and my wee black box as well."

"You should have kept the wee box with you," said the second old cailleach. "We knew by our spells that it was gone. 'Tis why we came."

"The king got hold of the box and used it to carry the castle and his daughter away," her sisters said.

"How could I be knowing he'd do the like? I'd not have thought it of a king!" said Ian Beg. "Och, well, 'tis my own fault for being careless. The castle's gone and the lass is gone, and without the box I cannot get them back again, so there's naught I can do about it. I'll go back to my father and help him in the bakehouse."

"Och, do not talk so daft!" said the third old cailleach. "You must go after them and bring the lot of them home."

"What luck would I have at that," asked Ian Beg, "and me not even knowing where they've gone?"

"That we can tell you," said the old cailleachs. "It's over the sea to the Island of the Kingdom of the Rats the castle and the king and his daughter have gone."

"In that case it might as well be behind the world's end for all that I can do," said Ian Beg.

"You're forgetting one thing," the third old cailleach

told him. "Am I not here to help you, and me still beholden to you for my share of your cake?" So she took Ian Beg by the hand and pulled him up to his feet, and led him away until they came to the shore of the sea.

"You'll be needing a ship," she said. And looking about her, she picked up a piece of driftwood that lay nearby on the sands. She tossed it out upon the waves and at once it became a fine ship.

"Now you'll be needing a captain to chart your course and steer your ship," she said. She looked about her again and saw a great black cat on the shore catching a fish for his supper, so she picked him up and threw him upon the deck of the ship.

"You shall be captain," she told the cat, "and sail the ship."

So the cat sat up straight in the captain's place, waiting the word to go.

"Now heed me well, Ian Beg," said the third old gray cailleach. "When you get to the Island of the Kingdom of the Rats, do not set foot from the ship, but send the cat to get the box and bring it to you. And when you have it safe in your hands again, you will know what to do."

Then Ian Beg thanked her for her help, and bade her farewell, and joined the cat on the ship. The cat sailed the ship well, and in good time they came to the place in the sea where the Island of the Kingdom of the Rats lay, and there Ian Beg saw his castle rising up high and proud a short piece up from the shore. The cat brought the ship up to a wharf of stones and anchored it, and Ian was just about to step off the ship, when he remembered what the old cailleach had said. So he told the cat to go up to the castle and find his wee black iron box and bring it back to him.

The cat jumped out of the ship, and the first thing he saw was a huge rat sitting at the end of the wharf, fishing with its tail for a line. The cat, being hungry, pounced on the rat and held him down, intending to have him for his supper.

"Nay!" said the rat, trembling with fear from his whiskers to the tip of his tail. "Pray do not eat me! Spare my life and I will help you. I know this kingdom better than you will ever know it, and if there is anything I can get for you I will gladly do so."

The cat held the rat down while he thought the offer over. At last he said, "It's a wee black iron box I'm wanting, and from what I hear it's somewhere in that castle up there. Have you seen it anywhere about?"

"That I have!" cried the rat. "As I came by the castle not long ago, such a box lay on one of the window sills near the road. Let me go and I'll fetch it for you."

So the cat released the rat and away he ran. Soon the rat came back with the box and gave it to the cat, who carried it to Ian Beg. Ian Beg opened the box and out jumped the three spry lads crying, "Easgadh! Easgadh! Ready! Ready! What will you have us do for you?" And Ian Beg wasted no time in telling them what to do.

"Carry my castle back to the place in the wood where it belongs, with the king's daughter and the king in it, too," he told them. "And let one of you make sure to beat the king well, all the way back, for making you bring my castle here."

So the three spry lads jumped off the ship and the cat jumped on, and the cat sailed the ship back home.

When they got back to Barra, Ian Beg got off the ship and started out to walk back to the wood in which he had built his castle. The cat got off the ship, too, and went to catch a fish for his supper, and what became of the ship nobody knows. Ian walked up the road along by the burn, and through the glen, and came at last to the wood, and there was his castle, standing tall and proud among the trees again.

In front of the castle were the three old cailleachs and the three spry lads, and the king, who was looking a bit battered and dazed from the beating he'd got for taking the castle away. And, best of all, there was the king's daughter herself, running to meet him and to welcome him home.

So the king's daughter married the son of the baker of Barra, and a very grand wedding it was. The king kept his promise and gave the young couple his blessing. He could not do less, for he knew that his son-in-law had in his pouch the wee black iron box that had the three spry lads within it, and the king had no wish to make their acquaintance again.

The wedding lasted for a week and a month and a day, and the guests came from far and near. There were so many guests at the wedding that both the king's castle and Ian Beg's were filled with folk. And who came to the wedding but the three old cailleachs, and they sat at the table with Ian Beg, who showed them every kind attention he could. There was music and dancing and feasting from morn till morn, and, for those who wanted to hear them, there were tellers of tales and those with their wallets full of such stories as you ne'er heard before. It was from one of them that I got this story that I've just told you about the son of the baker of Barra who married the king's daughter, and the two of them lived happily in Ian Beg's castle, all the rest of their days.

The Clever Lad from Skye

THERE was once a lad, Tormod MacLeod his name was, and he was one of the clan of MacLeods that lived on the Isle of Skye. Being the least one of a family of ten, his father had little to give him, so Tormod took it into his mind to go over to the mainland to make his fortune in one of the big towns there. He wandered from place to place until he came to Glasgow, and there he was lucky enough to find himself a place with a blacksmith who had need of a pair of hands to help him. As Tormod was willing and able he did well at the work, and his master being satisfied with him, he settled down to learn the trade.

He was so quick and clever at his work that the black-smith often blessed the day he came.

But if Tormod's hand was quick, his wits were quicker. There was little that happened about the town that he missed. As he had come over from Skye to make his fortune, he had his eye out to find a chance to do the same.

There was a Glasgow gentleman who had a horse that he was terribly fond of, and with justice, for it was a very fine steed. The gentleman brought it into the smithy one day to have it shod, and the blacksmith gave the job to Tormod to do. While Tormod was shoeing the creature he said to the gentleman, "That's a grand horse you have there."

"Aye, that it is," the gentleman said.

"What will you take for the beast?" asked Tormod.

"There's no amount of money could buy him," the gentleman said. "I'd not part with him for any amount of gold."

"Are you not afraid some thieving body will come along and carry him off, and him so valuable?" Tormod asked.

The gentleman laughed loud at that. "It could not be done," said he. "Och, he has his own stable to stay in, with four strapping big fellows to guard him, and with bells and gongs and horns to give the alarm and bring more, should anyone try to take him away."

"Och, away with your guards and bells and gongs and all!" scoffed Tormod. "And with your big fellows, too. I could steal him out of your stable if I had a mind to, before another week was out. And you'd know naught about it until you found him gone!"

At that the gentleman grew angry. "I've a hundred pounds here in my pocket that says that you cannot get him out of my stable without getting caught at it," he shouted. "Och, if you manage to do it, you may keep the horse!"

"D'ye mean that?" Tormod asked.

"Aye, and I do!" the gentleman said.

Then Tormod turned to the blacksmith who was standing by with his ears and his mouth wide open, and bade him witness that the gentleman had agreed that if Tormod could get the horse out of the gentleman's stable and into their own without getting caught at it, he was to have the horse to keep and a hundred pounds in money beside. So the bargain was made, and then the gentleman went off with his horse, which by this time was well shod, and Tormod went on with his work.

Tormod was not the sort of lad to slack his work, but when his day at the smithy was over he went off on his own. Up to the gentleman's house he went, to see how the land lay. Spying around, he found that it was just as the gentleman said. Behind the gentleman's house there was a tidy wee stable away from the big one, with a courtyard of its own, and there were four great strong ghillies watching the horse, and tending to it, and along the walls of the stable there were bells and gongs and horns galore, to give the alarm if help was needed. All that did not discourage Tormod in the least.

Well, the horse stayed safe in his stable, and Tormod stayed in the smithy for the first few days of the week. But on the fourth day Tormod made ready to take away the gentleman's horse. He had noticed that when the gentleman was away from home, riding upon his fine horse, the four ghillies were usually found at the tavern near the smithy, and from what Tormod had seen of them, he thought the lot of them were fonder of drinking than they ought to have been. "Och, well," said Tormod, "their weakness will be my strength."

That night he went to the tavern and bought three bottles of good strong drink. He put one in the pocket on either side of his jacket, but the third he kept in his hand. When he got to the gentleman's house he poured a bit from the bottle on to his clothes, then corked the bottle up again. He went around the house and into the courtyard of the stable where the fine horse was kept. He could see, through the open door, the four fellows tending to the horse by the light of a lantern that hung by its stall.

Tormod began to stagger about the courtyard, waving his bottle and singing foolish snatches of song, and muttering to himself. The four ghillies came running to find out what the commotion was, and as the first one came from the stable Tormod pretended to fall upon the ground as if he had slipped into a drunken sleep. There he lay, snoring and groaning loud enough to wake the dead. The four fellows bent over him scolding and shaking him, but he paid them no heed and only snored the louder. "Och!" said one of the ghillies. " 'Tis naught but a drunken lout that's strayed into the place. Pah! He fair reeks o'whuskey!" said he, as he got a whiff of the liquor Tormod had spilled on his clothes.

"Leave him be," said another. "He'll be able to do no harm the way he is, and when he comes round to himself in the morn, we'll hustle him out."

Then a third man saw the bottle of whiskey in Tormod's hand. "He'll have no need for this," he said, reaching down and taking the bottle away. "And we can very well use it."

So back to the stable they went to share the bottle among them. Tormod remained lying on the stones of the courtyard, pretending to be asleep.

When the bottle was empty, one of the ghillies said to the others, "That was well enough in its way, but it gives one a thirst for more. I'm thinking I felt another bottle in his pocket when I shook him." So they trooped out and felt in Tormod's pocket and there they found the second bottle, which they took back and shared, too. By the time the second bottle was empty every man of them was terribly unsteady upon his legs, and not as steady in his head as he should have been, but they were still thirsty. So out they went and found the last of the bottles Tormod had brought. By this time they'd never have known if Tormod was asleep or not, and when the last bottle was empty they had entirely forgotten that he was there. One by one, they settled down on the stable floor and fell asleep.

Tormod lifted his head to watch them, and when all four were snoring loudly, he leaped to his feet and went into the stable.

"Losh!" he said. "If with all that music you lads are making you do not wake each other, nothing that I do will rouse you, to be sure!" So he went boldly over to the horse and bridled and saddled it, and got up on its back. Then he rode out of the stable and out of the courtyard and down the road, and never stopped until he got back to the smithy. There he put the horse in a stall in the blacksmith's stable, and then he went to bed.

The gentleman came down to his stable in the morning to get his fine horse, intending to ride out upon it, to take the early fresh air. When he found the horse gone and the ghillies lying asleep on the floor of the stable he flew into a rage. He roused the ghillies by throwing a pail of cold water upon them, but even then they were so dazed and drowsy that they could tell him nothing at all. But the gentleman had no need to be told, for a moment's thought told him that Tormod MacLeod, the blacksmith's helper, had gotten away with his horse. So he had one of his other horses saddled, and it was much inferior to the fine one he'd lost. Off he galloped to the smithy. Tormod was there, and the blacksmith with him, both busy at their day's work. The horse was there, too, in the blacksmith's stable, contentedly eating some oats.

"You thief! You rogue!" the gentleman cried. "The sheriff shall take you up this day and jail you for stealing my horse."

"Not so fast!" Tormod said calmly. "I did not steal your horse, as you well know. Did we not make a bargain that if I could take the creature out of the stable without being caught, then I might keep it, with the blacksmith standing as witness when the bargain was made?"

"Aye!" said the blacksmith, well pleased to have such a clever lad as his helper. "And there was the matter of a hundred pounds, to boot, which I will thank you to hand over to the lad."

The gentleman fussed and fumed but there was naught he could do about it. The blacksmith stood firm. A bargain was a bargain. So in the end the gentleman had to put a hundred pounds of good money in Tormod's hand. "You'll ne'er get the better of me again!" the gentleman said, glowering at Tormod as he paid over the money.

"I'd not say that," said Tormod. "They tell me you've a bonnie young daughter that you're wanting to wed to a rich old laird. I hear that the lass does not see eye-to-eye with you about it, so you're keeping her pent up in her room until she changes her mind and agrees to wed the old coof. I've half a mind to go and get her and marry her myself!"

The gentleman nearly burst with rage. When he could speak, he said, "You ne'er could do so! I've got her shut up in a room at the top of the house, and from the front door to the door of the room she's in there are sluaghs of servants to make sure she doesn't run off before I get her wed to the laird."

"Och, the poor lass!" said Tormod. "But I could take

her out of the house just the same, with nobody stopping me the while I did so."

"If you can get her out and not be stopped, you may have her and welcome," the gentleman told Tormod. "But I have five hundred pounds of good money here in my pocket that says you cannot do it."

"Is it a bargain?" Tormod asked.

The blacksmith stepped up then and said to the gentleman. "Come now, have a care, for my helper here is a clever fellow, and what he says he's going to do, he's not likely to leave undone. You could lose your daughter to him, and your money as well." But the gentleman would not heed the blacksmith's good advice.

"Aye!" he said. " 'Tis a bargain!"

So the blacksmith stood again as witness to a bargain between the gentleman and Tormod. The way the bargain stood was, if Tormod could take the gentleman's daughter out of his house, and not be caught at it, he might marry the lass if he liked, and have five hundred pounds of the gentleman's money forbye!

Then the gentleman went away, and the blacksmith and Tormod got busy at their day's work.

Carrying off the gentleman's daughter was not going to be as easy as taking his horse had been. It took Tormod a fortnight to think how it could be done.

"The gentleman's fashing himself about the way you're going to steal his lass," the blacksmith told Tormod one day. "He's given out word that his daughter will be wedding the auld laird he's picked for her, and he's set the date of the wedding day."

Tormod only grinned at the blacksmith's news, for his plans were made, and he thought it very unlikely the gentleman's daughter would be marrying anyone but himself. So he took the next day off from his work, with his master's leave, and went off to the town's best dressmaker. There he so coaxed and beguiled her that she consented to sell him the gown and the bonnet that she was accustomed to wear as she went on her errands about the town, and the shawl and skirt and apron of the maid who usually accompanied her when she went out, as well. That wasn't all he got from her, for he cajoled her into lending him one of the big wicker dress-baskets that she used for carrying the fine garments she made to her customers, and she even found him a couple of caddies to carry the dress-basket for him, too. Although she bridled at his boldness, and said he had a great cheek to behave so sly, she gave him everything he wanted, and never asked what he was going to do with what she gave him.

Tormod had a good friend who was willing to help him. He had set his friend to watching the gentleman's house to discover when the gentleman would be going away from the town. Tormod's friend came back the very day that Tormod went to the dressmaker's house, and brought good news. "The gentleman's off and away," he told Tormod, "and he'll not be back this day again, for he has taken his luggage with him. Where he went to, I was not able to learn."

"Where he went to does not matter at all," said Tormod. "As long as he is not at home."

So Tormod got into the dressmaker's gown, and put her bonnet on his head, with a veil to hang down from it, and cover his face. The friend put on the maid's skirt and apron, and arranged the shawl over his head so as to hide his face. Then the two of them came out of the house where Tormod lived, and there were the caddies, waiting in the street, with the dress-basket, ready to go. Tormod started up the road toward the gentleman's house, and Tormod's friend followed him, walking respectfully a little behind him, and at the end of the procession came the two caddies carrying the wicker hamper between them. All the people they met on the way nodded or bowed, for they thought it was the dressmaker and her servant, whom they knew well, so good was their disguise. And Tormod nodded and bowed back, very well pleased with the success of his plan as far as it had gone. "May it go well to the end!" said Tormod to himself.

When they got to the house of the gentleman, Tormod knocked at the door. A servant opened it to him and Tormod spoke to him, making his voice high and mincing, and so much like the dressmaker's that if she had heard it, she'd have thought it was herself that spoke. "I've come to try the wedding dress on the gentleman's daughter," Tormod said. "There's very little time left ere the wedding day, and the fitting of the gown is important, in case there are changes that must be made."

"Och, aye!" said the servant. "Well, ye've been here

before, so you'll be knowing the way. The lass is on the top floor, in the room at the head of the stairs." Then he left them to find their own way, and went about his work.

So up the stairs the lot of them went, Tormod first, in the dressmaker's gown, then his friend in the maid's clothes, with the two caddies, bearing the hamper, coming along behind. Many a servant they passed on their way, but not one of them gave them a second glance. Och, the servants all thought as they passed by. 'Tis naught but the seamstress and her lass.

When Tormod came to the room at the top of the stairs, he opened the door and they all went in. After the caddies had set the dress-basket down in the middle of the floor, Tormod told them to wait in the hall outside until they were needed again, because it would not be seemly for them to stay in the room while the lady was changing her gown. So out they went, and Tormod shut the door behind them.

The lass whirled around from the window where she had been standing looking down at the street. Her eyes and her poor little nose were red from weeping, but still she was bonnier than any lass that Tormod had ever seen. Thinking Tormod was the dressmaker herself, the lass stamped her foot. "You may just take the gown away," said she. "For I'll ne'er wear it. I've said it before and I'll say it again. I will not marry that silly old laird!"

"You'll not, to be sure," said Tormod, speaking to her

with his own voice. "Have I not come to make sure that you do not?" And he took off the dressmaker's bonnet and veil and laid them aside.

When the lass saw that it was a man who wore the dressmaker's gown, she started back in terror. It was lucky for Tormod that she was too frightened to find her voice and scream, and bring the servants on the run. But Tormod talked to her so kindly and so gently that soon she listened to what he said. When she understood that he had come to save her from wedding the rich old laird, she was willing to do whatever Tormod told her to do. So Tormod popped her into the dressmaker's hamper and fastened the top down tight. Then he called the caddies and told them he was ready to leave. When the caddies came in from the hall and picked up the hamper, Tormod was at the mirror, fixing the veil of the bonnet, which he had put on again. If the caddies noticed the lass was not in the room they asked no questions about her, and if the hamper seemed heavier going out than coming in, they did not mention that at all. Out of the room they all went, Tormod with his bonnet and his veil hiding his face, then his friend, well-muffled in the maid's shawl, and last of all, the two caddies bearing the wicker hamper between them. They went down the stairs and all the servants they passed looked at them quickly and looked away again. "Och," they said to themselves. " 'Tis naught but the seamstress and her serving maid, going back home again."

When they got down to the front door, there was the

servant who had let them into the house. He opened
the door for them and as they went out of the house,
he bade them a polite "Good e'en," and then he closed
the door after them, and there was not one of the
servants who had seen Tormod that day who had not
been well fooled by the clever lad.

Tormod lost no time in leading his crew back to the
smithy. When they got there Tormod bade the caddies
to set the hamper down, saying that there was a strap
with a buckle that wanted mending. The blacksmith
would take care of it, and see that the hamper got home
safe when the job was done. He paid them for their
trouble and they ran off very well pleased with what he
gave them, and Tormod called to the blacksmith, who
came out of the smithy and gave him a hand. They
carried the dress-basket in and set it down on the floor,
and Tormod unfastened the straps and lifted up the
cover. There lay the lass, as snug as a kitten in a basket,
and not in the least harmed by her travels, and when
Tormod held out his hands to her, she sprang up and
out of the basket into Tormod's arms. Then he asked if
she would wed him, instead of the old laird, and she
said she was willing, so off they went to the priest that
very night. So Tormod married the gentleman's
daughter, as he had said he would, and the blacksmith
and Tormod's friend stood up with them as witnesses
when they were wed.

The next day the gentleman came home from wherever he had been and found the house in a terrible
state. The gentleman's daughter had disappeared the

day before, and, for the life of them, none of them could say how she got away. 'Twas not by the hall, for some of them had been watching there all the day. 'Twas not by the window, for that was too high, and there was naught she could climb down by. They'd searched the house from top to bottom, and she was not hiding anywhere within it. However she got away, she was gone, and that they'd swear to, for there wasn't a sight or a sound of her to be found.

The gentleman was so angry that sparks fair flew from his eyes. The first thing that came into his head was the bargain that he had made with the blacksmith's lad.

"Was there a great lout came to the house here yesterday?" he asked.

"Och, nay," the servants said. "There was not. De'il a body come to the hoose the whole day long," they told him. "That is, except for the dressmaker with her maid, who came to try the wedding gown on your lass."

"Wedding gown!" said the gentleman. "There's been no wedding gown ordered as yet. De'il take you all for a pack o' fools! I'll warrant that it was not the dressmaker yesterday at all, but the blacksmith's helper decked out in the dressmaker's clothes, and by some trick he's spirited my lass away."

Away to the smithy he rushed, and there were the blacksmith and Tormod, as busy as busy could be. There was his daughter, too, smiling and happy, watching the men as they worked. The gentleman made for his daughter, shouting, "Och, you graceless hizzy, come home wi' me now! I'll promise you'll not get away again, until I've seen you wed to the laird."

But Tormod stepped between the lass and her father, and would not let him come near her.

Then the blacksmith spoke up. "A bargain's a bargain," said he. "The agreement between the two of you was made plain and fair, and although I warned you against it, you would have your own way. The bargain was that if my helper could take your daughter out of your house without being caught, then he could keep her. And as he has done so, to my way of thinking the lass belongs to him."

Then the lass told her father, "I cannot marry your rich old laird, anyway, because I'm already married to Tormod here."

Well, the gentleman had to admit that Tormod had got the better of him again. But there was more misfortune to come for him.

"There's a little matter of some money ye're owing the lad," the blacksmith said, picking up a monstrous big sledge hammer from the anvil against which it was leaning, and hefting it thoughtfully in his hand. "Five hundred pounds, it was, and I'll be thanking you to pay it to him without delay."

The gentleman looked at the sledge hammer and then he looked at the blacksmith, who was eying him in a fashion he did not care for at all. There was naught he could do but take out his purse and pay the five hundred pounds into Tormod's hand.

"Make the most of it!" he growled. "For you've got

the best o' me for the last time," and he turned his back and walked away from them all.

Then Tormod, grinning all over his face, called after him. "Och, I'd ne'er say that. Why, I could take yourself out of your own house, as easy as I did your horse and your daughter, and you coming with me as easy and gentle-like as a led lamb."

The gentleman spun around on his heel and back he came to the door of the smithy. "Ye're daft!" said he. "I would not come willingly with you the length of six paces from my front door."

"Aye, but I could," Tormod said.

"Och, now," said the smith to the gentleman. "Have ye no sense at all? This business has gone far enough. Can you not see that you are no match for this clever lad o' mine? Whatever he says he'll do, I promise you, he'll be bound to do it. Leave it alone and make no more bargains with him!"

But the blacksmith might have saved his breath to cool his porridge, for all the good he did. The gentleman was not to hold or to bind.

"There's a thousand pounds in my kist at home that says you can never do so!" he shouted, brandishing his fist at Tormod. "If you can make me go anywhere with you, and me willing to go, you may have the gold."

"Is it a bargain, then?" asked Tormod.

"A bargain it is!" the gentleman said.

"Och, well," sighed the blacksmith. "If ye'll not see reason, I'll be witness to it again."

So it was agreed that if Tormod could make the

gentleman come out of his house and go with Tormod willingly, Tormod could have the gentleman's money and welcome to it, so the gentleman said.

Well, the days went by and turned into weeks, and weeks turned into months. The lass was happy and Tormod was happy and all went well. It might have been thought that Tormod had forgotten the bargain he had made with the gentleman, and as for the gentleman, the matter had slipped completely from his mind. But Tormod had not forgotten. He was just biding his time.

Well, at the turn of the year there was going to be a grand celebration in the town to honor some person of great distinction who was visiting there. There was going to be a big dinner, with all the gentry invited, and among the guests who were asked to attend was the gentleman whose horse and whose daughter Tormod had stolen away. When Tormod heard about it, he laughed loud and long. This was the sort of chance he'd been waiting for all this time.

Tormod started to get ready long before the day. In the first place, he had to persuade his wife to pay a visit to his mother on Skye.

" 'Tis a sin and a shame the two of you have had no chance to get acquainted," he told her. "Och, she's always begging me to send you to see her, and it would not look well to put it off any longer. She'll be thinking you're not wanting to know her, you see."

So his wife consented to go to the Isle of Skye and stay until the New Year for the Hogmanay holiday and maybe a fortnight or two longer, until Tormod came to fetch her home. But it was not so much to please his mother that Tormod wanted her to go, as it was that Tormod knew full well that his wife would ne'er put up with the trick he intended to play on her father, so it was best to keep her out of the way.

When she had gone, Tormod began to lay his plans for taking the gentleman away with him. He could count on the help of the blacksmith and the friend who had aided him before, but he'd be needing more than the two of them this time. He'd be needing a couple of fellows with trumpets, and maybe a dozen young caddies who looked to be lively and full of fun. He found them without too much bother, and gathered them together at the smithy, and a spry lot of *gavallachans* they were, to be sure. He had chosen them wisely, for they were just the lads to be ready for a bit of fun. When they heard what Tormod was up to, there was not one of them who would not have done his best at the job, without being paid for his trouble at all. It tickled them well to be playing a trick on a gentleman of the town, and such a fine gentleman, too. So Tormod set the date and the hour for them to meet him again and sent them on their way.

When the night of the great celebration came, all the lairds and the gentry of the town assembled about the table in the grand hall where the dinner was being held, and brave and bold among them, to be sure, was the gentleman whom Tormod was going to carry away. While the fine folk were feasting and passing the wine around the table, Tormod and his rascals were gathered together at the smithy, where Tormod was making certain that each man knew the part he must play.

One of the caddies had been sent to watch outside the hall, ready to bring word to Tormod when the dinner was over, and now he came running to say that the gentry were coming out of the hall. Tormod had managed to persuade the dressmaker to make him two long white robes with hoods to them, such as the old monks used to wear. One of these he put on himself, and folded the other over his arm. The blacksmith and the friend were left at the smithy to prepare for his return, while Tormod went off to the gentleman's house, taking his two trumpeters and the pack of caddies along with him.

'Twas the dark of the moon and the winter's night was black and cloudy, with never the twinkle of a star to be seen in the sky. When they got to the place, Tormod sent his companions to hide themselves nearby where they would not be seen. Tormod himself crouched behind a bush in the little garden, just outside the front door.

As soon as the gentleman turned toward his house door, Tormod was after him, stealing along close behind, so silently that the gentleman never knew he was there. When the gentleman opened his front door and went into his house, Tormod slipped in with him, and what with it being so dark, and with the gentleman paying no heed because his thoughts were taken up with the evening's pleasures, Tormod had no trouble at all getting past him into the house and taking his stand at the foot of the stairs. The gentleman felt around until he found a candle on a table against the wall in the hall, and having lit the candle, he turned to go up to his bed. His jaw dropped and his eyes goggled, for there at the foot of the staircase stood a tall figure all in white from head to foot. The gentleman took the apparition to be a ghost, and it scared what wits he had left clean out of his head.

"What's that!" he asked, his voice shaking with fright.

Tormod, standing tall in his long white robe, lifted an arm and pointed at the gentleman. "Wretched mortal!" he said, making his voice so deep and loud that it rumbled through the hall. "I have come to warn you! The end of the world is at hand and you must suffer judgment for the evil you have done in this world."

"Och, nay! Nay!" the gentleman cried, and his knees began to shake. "I am not ready to be judged yet."

"Ready or not," said Tormod sternly. "You'll be judged just the same."

"I've been none so bad," the gentleman wept, and he began to beg for help. "Och, if you are one of the blessed saints, as I take it you are, can you not save me?"

"I can not stay with you," Tormod said. "Soon the trumpets of doom will be blowing, and I shall be needed elsewhere."

"Take me with you, then," the gentleman pleaded. "I shall be safe if I am by your side."

"Happen you would," said Tormod doubtfully. "That

is, if the fiends did not come and drag you away from me. They'd know you at once upon seeing you, you may be sure."

"Oh, woe, woe!" wept the gentleman. "Save me, save me, blessed one!"

"Och, well—poor soul, I'll do what I can," said Tormod. "But are you willing to put yourself in my hands, and come with me?"

"Willing!" the gentleman said. "Och, and that I am! I'll go gladly where'er you take me."

"You'll not get far, clad as you are" said Tormod. "But here is a robe like my own. You and me will look the same as two peas out of the same pod when you get into it, and it will suit you fine for a disguise." And Tormod took the second white robe that he carried folded over his arm, and bundled the gentleman into it, taking care to pull the hood well down over the gentleman's face. "It will be best if they cannot make out who you are at all," Tormod said. "Lest they lay hands upon you to punish you for your sins."

The gentleman agreed to that, but if his face could not be seen, neither could he see. He groped about with his hands, trying to feel his way. "Give me your hand," said Tormod. "I'll lead you. My eyes will do for the two of us, never fear."

So the gentleman put his hand into Tormod's and off they started. The moment the two stepped out of the house the trumpeters in the garden let out a mighty blast on their horns, as Tormod had arranged that they should do.

"Och! Heaven save us! What's that?" shrieked the gentleman, frantically clutching Tormod's arm in his fright.

" 'Tis the Angel Gabriel, blowing the trump o' doom," said Tormod. "He'll be marking the beginning of the Judgement Day."

Then on all sides there was the sound of screeching and wailing, and fleeing feet and wild laughter. Tormod had to half carry and half drag the gentleman along the road, he was so weak with fright. With his eyes covered by the folds of the heavy cloth of the hood the poor wretch could see not a thing, but that was satisfactory to him, for he had no wish to see. To hear was bad enough, to his mind.

At last they reached the smithy and Tormod led the gentleman inside. The blacksmith and Tormod's friend were there, throwing fuel on the fire by the forge until it blazed nearly to the roof. There was such a clashing and glee-glashing of iron as you never heard in your life, as they knocked pokers and hammers and shovels together, while the shouting and shrieking of the caddies outside came nearer and nearer all the time. Although the gentleman could not see, he could feel the heat, and hear the crackling and roaring of the fire above the uproar outside the smithy.

"Och!" he cried out to Tormod. "In heaven's name, what are those awful sounds? What is that terrible heat I feel?"

" 'Tis the flames of the fiery pit you're feeling," Tormod said. "And the noise is the gates of doom as they open and close, and the shrieks of the poor lost sinners as they are carried in."

Then Tormod said to the gentleman, "I can stay no longer. I must be on my way. Before I go I will take you to a place where, if you truly repent your sins, you will, no doubt, be safe."

Then he led the gentleman past the fire and into the wee room behind the forge where the horses' food and other stores were kept. The gentleman fell on his knees on the floor, and Tormod left him kneeling there, saying his prayers.

All night long the blacksmith and Tormod's friend kept the fire roaring high and the fire irons crashing, and all night long the trumpeters and the caddies shrieked and screamed and leaped about the blacksmith shop. Why the neighbors did not send for the sheriff because of the wild carouse I cannot tell you, but happen Tormod had made it all right with them in advance. When daybreak came, Tormod called a halt to the racket, and laid his white robe aside. The blacksmith and Tormod's friends let the fire go down, and the trumpeters and the caddies left off their shrieking and gamboling, and were not sorry to do so, for they were fair winded by that time. Tormod paid them all well, for they had earned it, and sent them home.

It was suddenly very still in the blacksmith shop. Tormod opened the door of the storeroom. There was the gentleman still kneeling on the floor, in the white robe that Tormod had clad him in, and with the hood still well over his face.

"Och, you can come out now," Tormod said.

The gentleman recognized Tormod's voice, and for a few minutes he stayed as he was, stock still. Then he pushed the hood from his face and looked about him and saw the sacks of corn, and the hides and nails and suchlike things that were stored in the wee room. He got to his feet slowly, rubbing his knees which were stiff from the night's long kneeling, and then he walked past Tormod, out of the storeroom into the smithy, and all the time he said not one word.

"Well, and did I take you out of your house?" asked Tormod.

"You did," the gentleman said.

"And did you come with me willingly?" asked Tormod.

"I did," the gentleman said. And then, without another word, he walked out of the smithy, still wearing the long white robe, and home he went.

Neither the gentleman nor Tormod said a word about making another bargain between them. That day, before noontide, the gentleman's man of business came to the smithy and gave Tormod a bundle, and when Tormod opened it up he found in it the white robe the gentleman had worn, and the thousand pounds that Tormod had won.

But that is not the end of the story. Tormod fetched his wife back from Skye, and now that his mischief was over, Tormod told her what he had done to her father on Hogmanay night. Very vexed she was, too, but in the end she said that happen it would teach her father to stop trying to get the best of Tormod with his old bargains, which would be a very good thing, for she did not hold with betting and gambling forbye. And if Tormod would promise to play no more tricks upon her poor old father, she supposed she'd have to forgive him this time.

Early one morn, a few days later, Tormod called his wife to him. "You know that fine horse I got from your father?" said he. "Well, now, you're to be taking it back to him, and tell him that I said 'twas a very grand creature, but that I do not care to keep it any longer, so he'd better have it back."

His wife looked surprised, but said nothing, and as she started away to get ready to go, Tormod called her back to him. "That's not all," said he. And into her hand he put fifteen hundred pounds, and that was the five hundred he had got when he carried her off, and the thousand the gentleman had sent after he had been carried off himself. As for the hundred pounds Tormod had got for carrying off the horse, he no longer had that, for the dressmaker and the two trumpeters and the caddies got all of that.

"Tell your father I thank him for the use of his money, but as I'm not needing it any more, he might as well have it, too." So his wife did as Tormod told her, and took the horse and the money back to the gentleman and told him what Tormod had said.

When their first child was born, and it a son, Tormod would have it no other way than that it should be called after his wife's father, which gave the gentleman a great deal of pleasure. It wasn't long after that that he was heard bragging that Tormod MacLeod, his son-in-law, was a very fine fellow, and there wasn't a man in all Scotland who could match him for cleverness. But of course he never told anybody why he thought the same.

As for Tormod, who had come all the way from the Isle of Skye to Glasgow to find his fortune, he was entirely satisfied. He had a good trade and a good master, a bonnie wife and a grand wee son—and what better fortune could any man want?

The Lass That Lost the Laird's Daughter

A lass once lived on a wee croft on the Isle of Arran, over the mountains from the castle of Brodick, and some way from the sea. A lonely place it was, but she did not lack for company for she was one of a large-sized family. Twelve bairns in all there were in the house, counting from herself, who was the oldest, down to the least one still in its cradle, to say nothing of her father and mother and the old grandam croodlin' o'er the fire. Thirty feet, all in the one wee house, pacing in and out and about, can stir up a lot of commotion, and what with the bairns chattering and laughing and greeting, and their elders talking loud to make themselves heard, it was enough to send a body fair distracted, so it was.

One day the lass stopped in the middle of the floor of the room, and looked about her and listened. "Lawks!" said she to herself. "A dozen weans fill the place up, and likely there will be more to come! I'd best do somewhat about it!"

So she went to her father and mother and told them she had a mind to be leaving them to go and see a bit of the world, and maybe do some good for herself.

"Och, you're o'er young to be fending for yourself," said her father.

"Aye," sighed her mother, "and you but such a wee thing, forbye."

"Young I may be but I'll soon grow older," said the lass. "And if I'm wee, I'm hale and strong. I have a good pair of willing hands, and you can make good use of the room I'm taking up now. So give me your blessing and I'll be on my way."

Well, her mother and father saw that her mind was set upon going, so they wasted no more words trying to hold her from it. Her father gave her a bit of money to put in her pocket and her mother made up a bundle with her Sunday gown, some aprons and a shift or two, and such other things as she'd need, and the old grandam gave her own Bible for the lass to take along. 'Twas all they had to give her but their blessing, and when she had that she started off on her own.

Over mountain and moor she went, traveling while the daylight lasted, and when night came, if a house was nearby she asked for shelter, and folk were kind and took her in. When there was no house to be seen she rolled herself in her shawl and slept in the heather or under a bush. At last she came to a town, and there it was market day, with a hiring fair at the end of the stalls, so she went and stood with the other lads and lasses who were waiting for somebody to come by and choose one of them to work for him. The other lads and lasses were the rough and pushing sort, with plenty to say for themselves when anybody came up to look them over. The lass said nothing at all, but stood quietly at the end of the line with her Bible under her arm.

Such a wee thing she was, and so quiet, forbye, 'tis a wonder she was noticed at all with such a noisy lot around her, but among the gentry there was a laird with his wife who were looking for a lass to be a house servant and give a hand to the cook. They liked the quiet, modest look of the lass, so they hired her in spite of her being so small, and carried her home in their carriage to their house which stood several miles away from the town on the other side of the moor.

The lass had no fault to find with the job, for although she was given plenty to do, the work was not hard, and she would be well paid when quarter day came around, at the end of each three months she worked, so she could count on sending some money home to her father and mother when her wages came due. She was well treated by all who dwelt under the laird's roof, so soon she felt at home and happy there.

The laird had only one child, a daughter, twelve years of age or thereabouts, and the bairn took a terrible fancy to the new serving maid. The daughter wanted to be wherever the lass was and followed her about the house as she worked. The chatter and laughter of the laird's daughter made the work seem lighter, so the lass did not mind having her company, but she took care not to let the bairn hold her back from her tasks, so that the laird and his lady, seeing how well her work was done, were pleased to let their daughter spend as much time with the lass as she liked.

When the lass had been at the laird's house a year, or maybe a bit more, the laird's wife had a new bairn, a wee son, and everyone in the place went about with such joy that one would have thought there had never been a babe born in the world before. The christening party was going to be such as had never been seen, with all the best that the larder could provide. The laird invited all the folk who lived within walking or riding distance to come, and such a hustle and bustle to get ready filled the house that the lass thought it was like being at home again with all the bairns there, and her mother and father and the old grandam croodlin' o'er the fire.

On the day before the christening party, the lass went into the kitchen shortly after noontide and found the cook with tears in her eyes and wringing her hands with vexation. "Och!" she said to the lass. "I cannot make the *beannachadh* bowl for the folk to drink the new bairn's health after the christening. I've used up the last bit of spice in the house for the cakes. The poor bairn will never thrive if folk do not drink his health in the proper way. My auld mither once went to a christening where there was no blessing bowl provided, and the poor bairn that was christened died within the year. And not a soul will oblige me by going to the town for the spices I need. I'd go myself, were I not needed so badly here."

"Och, now, hush your greeting!" said the lass. "I'll go fetch what you need myself. My work is done for the time, and I doubt they'll be needing me before I come home again."

"Och, ye'll not be wanting to walk so far," the cook protested. " 'Tis a long way to the town."

"I often walked farther to the church when I lived at home," said the lass. "Fetch the order from the master while I go tidy myself, and I'll be there and back again before you know I'm gone."

While the lass was combing her hair, the laird's daughter came seeking her, and seeing her getting ready asked where she was going.

" 'Tis only to the town I'll be going to fetch some spices for the cook," the lass said.

"Then I'll go with you," said the laird's daughter.

"Och, nay! 'Tis too far," said the lass.

" 'Tis not too far," said the laird's daughter.

"The master will not give you the leave to go," said the lass.

"I'll go ask him," the laird's daughter said, and off she ran, and soon came back to say that her father said he'd not mind her going at all, provided that the lass would see to it that she came home safe.

The lass would have been better pleased to be going without the laird's daughter, as it was in her mind that she'd travel faster alone, but since the laird had given his consent she did not like to gainsay him, so off to the town the pair of them went. The road was long but the laird's daughter was not bad at walking, to the lass's surprise. They came to the town in good time and found the shop where they sold the spices that the cook wanted for her beannachadh bowl.

It was after the spices had been measured out and wrapped up, and their cost set down to the laird's account, that the trouble began. The lass put the packet of spices in her pocket and came out of the shop, but when she turned to go homeward the laird's daughter would not go. Had she walked all this way, said she, only to go back home without so much as a glance at all the sights to be seen in the town? She did not get a chance to come to the town more than once in a twelvemonth, and now she was here she intended to make the best of the opportunity. The lass coaxed and begged, but it did no good at all. In the end there was naught for the lass to do but follow the laird's daughter as she roved through the town.

The laird's daughter saw no reason for haste, but ran hither and thither, looking at this and at that. It vexed the lass sorely, because time was passing by, and as it grew later and later she began to fash herself about the long road home, and to wonder if they would be able to travel it all before the fall of night. The hard cobblestones tired her feet, which were accustomed to go on country roads, and she did not like the way the town ladies, in their fine town gowns and their feather- and flower-trimmed bonnets, looked at her as they passed by. She thought they smiled with scorn at her plain coarse blouse and skirt and shawl, and it never occurred to her that they smiled with envy to see her bonnie fresh young face, with its bright eyes and rosy cheeks.

It was very near sundown before she managed to get her way, and turn the laird's daughter toward home. They started out on the road over the moor, but their feet did not step along so fast and so light as they had on their way to the town. Both the lasses were tired out with going to and fro through the streets. The light began to fail and the air grew cold and damp as they trudged in the gloaming along the track across the moor, and soon the laird's daughter began to lag behind and complain.

The lass tried to hurry her up. "Och, come now," she coaxed. " 'Tis but a mile and a bittock to go, and we'll be home again, and I'll lave your wee tired feet in cool water, and you shall have your supper and go to your bed."

But the laird's daughter would not be coaxed or hurried. "I can go no farther," she declared. A green grassy bank bordered the road with a wee hillock behind it, and throwing herself down upon the bank she told the lass that she'd not go one step forward until she had taken a bit of a rest. The lass was fain to go on by herself to the laird's house and have him send a pony to carry his daughter home, but the dusk would soon give place to night and she did not like to leave the laird's daughter alone in the dark. As there was naught else for her to do, she sat down under a rowan tree on the other side of the road to wait until the laird's daughter was ready to go on.

Until she sat down beneath the tree the lass had no notion of how weary she was. She would be none the worse for a bit of rest herself, she thought. So, until the laird's daughter was willing to take up the journey again, she made herself comfortable and easy by folding her arms upon her knees and laying her head upon them, and before she knew what was happening to her, she had fallen fast asleep.

Some hours later she was wakened by the sound of loud voices, and by a light shining in her eyes. She looked up in surprise to see the laird himself peering down at her, holding a lighted lantern in his hand. The laird had grown troubled when it grew dark and the lass did not come home with his bairn. He knew the countryside was safe, and there could be nothing to harm them, and it was not likely they'd go astray, the track over the moor being wide and well used. But still he felt uneasy as the hours went by and the lass and his daughter did not return. At last he sent for some of his ghillies who lived on the estate and bade them bring lanterns and come with him to search for the missing pair. Going along the road over the moor, the searching party had come upon the lass asleep at the side of the road.

"Where have you left my daughter?" the laird asked the lass.

"Left her?" answered the lass, bewildered. "Och, I have not left her at all! She's over the road on the grassy bank there, fast asleep."

"That she is not!" said the laird. "Look for yourself, and you'll see." And he turned the light of the lantern so that it shone upon the bank. It was the truth that he spoke, for there was not a sign of the lass to be seen.

"Och, the poor bairn!" the lass lamented. "She must have wakened in the darkness, and thought I had left her alone. But did she not come home by herself then?"

"She did not," said the laird. "Would I be seeking her if she had?"

Then one of the ghillies said that happen the laird's daughter had got herself turned about in the dark and started to walk back toward the town, thinking that she was going home, in which case she'd not be likely to have gone far, what with the dark and all. Let the laird go home with the serving lass, he said, to wait there for the bairn. He and his fellows would go back toward the town and search along the road that led over the moor.

Long after midnight the men came back and told the laird that they'd sought the road from end to end, to the town and back again, and there was no trace of his daughter to be found. She must have wandered out onto the moor, and lost herself there some place, they said.

"Och, well, leave it be for now," said the laird

wearily. "We cannot search the moor by night. Go home and get what rest you can now, and at the break o' dawn we'll take up the search again."

By the next day's dawn the laird had sent word around in all directions that there would be no christening party that day because his daughter was lost and he must find her. All the countryside turned out to help with the search. From end to end the moor, and every corrie and coppice and glen were hunted over by the laird and his companions, and even the folks who lived in the town, when they heard the bairn was gone, made sure that she had not taken shelter in any of the houses there. But all the searching was of no use at all, for not a trace of her was found. As day after day went by and the laird's daughter was not found, little by little the search was given up. Although they grieved with the laird and his lady, everybody felt that there was no use to go on seeking longer, leaving work that must be done.

"It is a rare queer thing, is it not now?" they asked each other, "for a good-sized lassie like that one to disappear and not a trace left behind her?" And they shook their heads, not understanding it at all.

Well, the months went by, and only the new little son was left to cheer the laird and his wife. The house was sad and silent and nothing seemed the same. Nobody blamed the lass for losing the laird's daughter, the laird and his lady least of all. The lass was treated as kindly as ever she was before. It was the lass who blamed herself for bringing such sorrow upon them. She had failed in her duty, she often said to herself, because the laird had put his daughter into her charge, and she had let her get lost.

Then, when the laird's daughter had been missing nine months or thereabouts, a rumor began to go about. There were some who said that it was not reasonable to believe that she could disappear, and not leave so much as a trace behind. They whispered, one to another, that the lass must have killed the bairn and buried her somewhere on the moor. When the gossip came to the laird's ears, as in time it did, he was terribly troubled about it. He did not believe a word of it, and bade the lass to pay it no heed at all. But folk went on talking, and when what was being said reached the ears of those who administered the law of the land, they took heed of it, for, they said, what so many were talking about often turned out to be true. They came and got the lass and took her away to prison, to hold her until she could be brought to trial.

The laird promised to do what he could for her, and his lady stood up for her, and told her to be a good lass and not to fret, for God would protect the innocent. But what good could the two of them do against such a weight of talk?

There was a young man of law in the town who took a great interest in the lass. No matter what folk told him, he would not believe that she had harmed the laird's daughter at all. How could she have done so, he asked them, with the laird's daughter a strapping strong bairn, almost as big as the lass. The bairn would have been more than able to give a good account of herself against a little thing like the lass. And would they tell him how could the lass find a place on the moor to hide the body in, and her without so much as a spade to dig the grave?

He went to those who had her in charge and offered to stand for her defense, when the case came to court, and although they were not convinced by what he said, they listened. The lass must come to trial, they told him gravely, but if he wanted to talk to her they would not stand in his way. So he took their order with him and went to talk to the lass.

When he had talked to her the young man of law was more certain than ever that she had done no wrong. She neither wept nor complained, and she looked at him with eyes that were so clear and honest, and there was such an innocent air about her, that he knew in his heart that she never could have done the terrible thing that people said she did. She answered all his questions but she had nothing to tell him. "How could I remember?" she asked him. "And me being fast asleep? But she was in my care, so it was all my fault."

The young man's heart sank within him, for he doubted if he could help her, but he put on a cheerful face and asked if there was aught he could do—carry a message to those who were anxious about her, or send word to her home?

"I have only one wish in the world," said she. "I doubt my father and mother will know what has happened to me, for they live some distance from this place. If I could only go to my own home again, to tell them, and bid my family good-by, I would ask nothing more. And if they gave me leave to go, I'd give my promise to come back again, and suffer whatever fate I must."

"Och, well, I'll do what I can," said he.

When he went back and told them what the lass wanted to do, they said at first that such a thing had never been done before, and they were surprised he'd ask it. But he kept after them and gave them no peace.

" 'Tis a little thing to grant the wee body," said the young man of law. "To see her father and mother, and it maybe the last time she'll do so in this world! And all because of something she never did at all. Look ye now, if she promises to come back, you need not fear she will not, for she's not the sort of a lass to break a promise. Och, if that is what bothers you, I'll take her place myself!"

Happen his offer persuaded them, or happen 'twas just that they had begun to doubt that the lass had done wrong after all. Whatever their reason, they sent for the lass and when she was brought before them, they told her that she might go home to say good-by, but she must come back as she promised before the day set for her trial.

The lass thanked them and gave them her word to return, and then she gathered together all the wee things that she owned, and as she had come, with her bundle in her hand and her grandam's Bible under her arm, she went back over moor and mountain, following the road, and came at last to her home.

They came running out to greet her with joy and drew her into the house. She stood stock still in the middle of the room and looked about her and listened, and it was all the same, except that there was a new bairn in the cradle, born since she went away. But all the rest of the bairns were in and out and about the place just as they were before, and the grown folk were talking loud to make themselves heard above the clamor the weans were making, and the old grandam sat croodlin' o'er the fire. The only thing different was in herself, for when she went from them her heart had been filled with hope, and now it was filled with sorrow.

The lass bade her mother send all the bairns out of the house for a bit, and to bid them not to come back until she called them. When they were gone, she shut the door and sat herself down by the table, and told them what had happened and why she had come home.

"All I took with me when I went out into the world, I have brought back again," she said. "And the money I've earned, forbye. And I've brought back my grandam's Bible, because I knew when she gave it to me, she gave me the only treasure she had. And now I must bid you all good-by and leave you."

Her mother and father wept and embraced her, begging her to stay with them and they would keep her safe. Nobody was likely to find her here, even if they came seeking, because they would hide her so well.

"Nay, I have given my word to return," said she. "I cannot break it. I must go back and bear whatever my fate may be."

Then the old grandam who sat croodling o'er the fire raised her head and looked at the lass. "The laird's daughter is safe and well," said she. "No harm has come to her. Take up your bundle and take the Bible with you, and go back the way you went the first time. But do not stop in the town, but set your feet on the road that leads over the moor to the laird's house, and when you get to the place where the laird's daughter laid herself down to rest, sit down upon the green grassy bank upon which she lay. When the time comes for you to act, your heart will tell you what to do. But not for a moment, whatever happens, let the Bible out of your hand. Keep a fast hold upon it, and all will be well!" So the lass went back again, as her grandam had bade her, over mountain and moor, with her bundle in her hand and her Bible under her arm. When she got to the town she did not stop there, but set her feet upon the road to the laird's house. When she came to the green grassy bank where she had last seen the laird's daughter lying, she sat herself down, and took her Bible into her hand. She opened it and read for a while until night began to draw in and she could no longer see the words on the page in the gloaming. She shut the Bible then, but as her grandam had bade her, she held it fast in her hand. Soon it was night, and she sat there in the dark, waiting, and indeed she did not know what she was waiting for, but it was what the old grandam had told her to do.

Then she heard a sound as of voices talking and laughing, and there were strains of music on the air.

"They must be having a *ceilidh* at the laird's house over beyond the moor," she said to herself.

But as she listened, it seemed to her that the music and laughter came from somewhere nearer than the laird's house, and it a mile and more away. Even in the still night it would not sound so loud if it came from there. Now that her ear was tuned to the music it was as if the sound came from the mound which rose up behind the bank upon which she sat. Something within her, and perhaps it was her heart telling her, as her grandam said it would, urged her to rise and follow the sounds. So up she got, with her Bible fast in her hand, and around the hillock she went to see. In the darkness, she would have seen nothing at all if it had not been for a narrow slit in the side of the mound through which a ray of light shone bright, and drawing nearer she made out a big flat stone which was set into the side of the hillock like a door. The stone fitted so poorly that a long narrow space was left between it and the earth in which it was fixed, and it was through this crack that the brightness came.

The lass set her eye to the crack to see what she could see, and there inside the hillock was a fine great hall lit by thousands of candles so that all was as bright as a sunny day. There were harpers and pipers and drummers making music, and a great sluagh of finely dressed ladies and gentlemen, laughing and singing and talking merrily as they danced. And there in the midst of them was the laird's daughter alive and hearty, and as happy as a bird! She was singing and dancing and having a gay old time with them all.

"Och, now I see the way of it all!" the lass cried out. " 'Tis the *Sidhe* of the green hill who have had the laird's daughter all this time!"

She tucked her Bible into her pocket and set her fingers to tugging and pulling at the stone until she had dragged it away. Then she took the book out of her pocket, and down she rushed into the hall and catching the laird's daughter by the hand, she pulled her out of the place. All the fine company came tumbling after them and tried their best to get the bairn away from the lass, but she held her Bible between the ladies and gentlemen, and herself and the bairn. They dared not come after and had to let her go, so they drifted away on the moonlight and soon disappeared. The lass hustled the laird's daughter up the road toward her father's house and she kept a tight hold on her hand every step of the way.

"Och," grumbled the laird's daughter. "You had no need to hurry me off so soon. I'd no more than got there, and a grand time I was having too. We'd no more than begun to reel. You might have let me finish it, at the least."

"Soon!" cried the lass. "Och, well, if you had no more than begun the reel in a twelvemonth's time, when do you think you would be finished with it, I'm wanting to know!" But then she saw by the bewildered look on the bairn's face that she had no notion at all of how long

69 .

she had been in the fairy hall, so she said no more.

When they got to the laird's house the lass rapped loud on the door, and the laird, startled, came to open it himself.

"There's your daughter," the lass said. " 'Twas the fairy folk who had her all this time, but I have brought her home to you safe and sound, as I should have done long ere this."

Then all the sorrow of the house was turned to joy and all the countryside rejoiced with the laird and his lady, because his daughter was found. The laird's daughter refused to believe that she had been gone, not one night, but a twelvemonth, until they showed her the wee brother. Then she saw with her own eyes that the newborn babe, that lay in the cradle the day she went to the town with the lass to buy spices for his beannachadh bowl, had grown to be a bonnie big laddie a year old.

The laird and his lady could not do enough for the lass after she fetched their daughter home. They took her into their family, and loved her and treated her as if she were a daughter of their own. There was no more talk of a trial, and the gentlemen who administered the law of the land admitted that they had all been wrong, which gave great satisfaction to the young man of law.

The lass was still a wee thing, for she added little to her height, but she had grown a year or two older since she first left her home. 'Twas what she had told her mother and father that she would do, but what she didn't tell them was what she did not know herself—that she would grow bonnier and bonnier with every passing year. So pretty soon the young man of law came along wooing her, and after a while the two of them were wed. And when she went to her new home as a young wife the dearest treasure that she had in the house was the Bible she got from the old grandam who sat croodlin' o'er the fire.

Three Fat Ewes for Three Fine Hounds

IN the old days a king once lived on the Isle of Mull who had two bairns, a lad and a lass, and they as different from each other as the day is to the night. The lad was shining and bright, with a smile that would take the heart from out of your breast, and eyes as blue as the skies on a cloudless summer's day. A kinder, friendlier lad never drew breath, and his own heart was as true as pure gold.

His sister was as dark as he was fair, with black sullen eyes and black hair, and her heart was as black as the deep dark pools that are hidden away in a peat bog. Castle folk used to fork their fingers behind their backs as she passed by, and whisper to each other that the king's daughter had the evil eye.

Well, the mother of the two bairns died and the king, their father, married again. The new stepmother had been a widow and had a brood of her own to begin with, and by the time a dozen years or more had gone by, she and the king had added to hers another brood of their own, and so soon the place was so full of bairns that a body could scarcely find room in it where he could set down a foot, and not be trampling on one or another of them.

The king's son did not mind at all that he had been given a sluagh of wee brothers and sisters, and liked them very well, but his sister was ill pleased to find the castle filling up so quickly with the new family. But when she carried her grievances to her brother, he only laughed. "Och, now!" he told her. "Are they not bonnie and biddable, and loving wee things? To my mind it's pleasant to have them about the place."

"Och, ye loon!" the king's daughter said fiercely. "Are you daft entirely? 'Twas well enough when there were but the two of us, for we were the heirs to all our father's holdings and his gold, but now we must share with the lot of them, and what we get in the end will be very much less."

"Och, do not fash yourself about it," said the king's son. "Our father is a just man, and he is far from poor. There will be enough for all of us, and each one will get his due."

But his sister would not be calmed by her brother's

words. She brooded in sulky silence, watching the king's new bairns with a louring eye. The stepmother soon saw that the king's daughter had no love for the bairns, and in her heart she began to fret lest the lass do them some harm. At last she could bear the worry no longer, so she went to her husband, the king, and told him of her fears.

"Och, aye," the king said. "I'd noticed it myself. Well, we'll send the lass to live with her mother's kinfolk. No doubt she'll be happier there than here."

But when they told the king's daughter what they intended to do with her she flew into a rage, and she put her foot down flatly and said she would not go.

"You shall not foster me on my mother's folk," she told them. "And myself to fetch and carry for them like a serving maid, no doubt. Liefer than that I'll go out into the world by myself to make my fortune, and no thanks to you!"

It was no use to tell her that her mother's kin would love her and welcome her gladly, and keep her as a daughter to cosset and pet.

"The sole of my foot and the back of my hand to the lot of them," she said roughly. "And as soon as tomorrow's morn breaks, I'll be on my way."

"Go, then!" the king cried angrily. "I'll not stand in your way."

"That I will!" his daughter said.

When the king's son saw that his sister was bound to go, he said that she should not go alone. It would not be seemly for a young lass, and she a king's daughter, to tread the roads alone. He would go with her, he said.

"Come if you like," the king's daughter said. "I have not asked you, and it's all one with me whether you stay behind or go with me. Please yourself."

The king would do nothing at all for them, saying that since they were leaving his roof to make their own way they could do so without any help from him. But the stepmother was a gentle woman and had naught to say against the king's children, nor did she wish them any harm. That they might not go empty-handed, she gave them a sack of meal, a packet of salt, and a bit of money she had of her own, and the three best ewes from the king's flock forbye, so that the world would see that she meant to do well by them.

Then, at the day's dawn, off went the king's dark daughter, and no blessing went with her, for the king would not give her his blessing and her stepmother's she would not take. And step for step, beside her, went the king's fair son, carrying the sack of meal and the packet of salt, and driving the three fat ewes before him.

The brother and sister walked the roads of the world until one day as night was falling they came to a clearing in a wood that grew at the foot of a tall green hill. In the clearing there stood an empty shieling with four stout walls, a good thatched roof, and a door to the front and one to the back of it. The king's son looked in at the door which stood open. "Bless the luck which brought us here!" he cried. "The place is not big, but it is not so small that the two of us cannot bide here together."

The king's daughter grumbled that it was not what she was used to, but she was wearied with walking, so she followed her brother into the house. They put the sack of meal and the salt on a shelf in one corner, and tethered the three ewes in another, and then the lad went out and gathered bracken and brought it in. The king's son took one of the remaining corners and the king's daughter the other, and making themselves beds of the bracken, they lay down and slept.

When morning came the sister rose and looked about her. Under the shelf where the meal bag sat she saw a kettle or two and a stone griddle which, no doubt, had been left behind by those who had last lived in the house. She woke her brother and, giving him one of the kettles, bade him go milk the ewes that they might have milk for their morning meal. Then she took the other kettle and fetched water from the burn that ran by, near the shieling, and mixing the water with some of the meal, she made bannocks and, putting them on the griddle, she built up a fire on the hearth and set the bannocks to bake.

When her brother came in with the milk she said to him scornfully, "Is it not a fine thing that a king's son and a king's daughter should bide in a wee thatched hut and toil for their bread like the poor folk on my father's land?"

"It will not always be so," said her brother. "Fortune will smile on us one of these days, maybe sooner than you know."

"Och, such blethering," his sister said. "Fortune showed her heels to the two of us the day our stepmother walked into our father's house."

Her brother found nothing to say to that, so he held his tongue, and when they had broken their long night's fast he took the three ewes and led them up the green hill to graze on the tender young grass, while he sat under a tree, watching to see that they did not go astray.

As he sat there keeping them under his eye a man came up the brae and stopped beside him. Three great staghounds followed the man, and when the man stopped, the dogs stopped, too, at his heels.

"Those are very fine fat ewes you have there," said the man to the king's son.

"They're well enough," the lad answered.

"They're nicely fleeced," said the man. "The wool looks both long and fine."

"Aye, they're none so bad," the king's son agreed. Then he looked at the dogs standing behind the man. "The hounds are well worth looking at, too," the king's son said.

"Aye, they're very good creatures, and each of them has a special gift of its own," the man admitted. "But I'm a crofter, not a huntsman, so they are of little use to me. I'd liefer have your three fat ewes to add to my flock than all the dogs that ever coursed the land. Would you consider making a trade, now? My three hounds for your three ewes?"

The lad thought it over and it was in his mind to accept the crofter's offer. "Och, I was ne'er born to be a shepherd, to tell you the truth," said he. "To be a huntsman would suit me fine. With your hounds to help me, my sister and I would never lack for food, and when the wee bit of money we have is gone, I doubt that the wool from out three ewes would sell for enough to keep us long alive. Aye, I'll take your hounds if you like, and you may have the ewes."

"Your choice is wise, if you're minded to be a huntsman," said the man. "The hounds will be of good service to you, for each one has an unusual quality which adds to its value, and makes it more useful than an ordinary hound. This one with the red collar is named Fios, or Wisdom, and he has all the knowledge in the world. If you heed him, you will never go wrong. The one with the blue collar is Luathas, or Swiftness, and he can outrun the wind. The third one, who wears the green collar, is named Gramalas, or Strength, and he is stronger a hundred times over than anything else in the world."

"The bargain suits me!" said the king's son. "And here's my hand on it."

"The bargain suits me, too," said the crofter, so the two of them clasped hands to seal the trade.

Then the crofter gathered the three ewes together and drove them over the hill before him, and the king's son called the dogs to him. They seemed to understand that they had changed masters, and came willingly, so he started back with them to the shieling, in the clearing in the wood at the foot of the hill, and very well pleased he was with the bargain he had made.

But his sister was not so pleased about it, for when he got home and told her that he had traded the ewes for the three hounds she nearly burst with rage. She did not say a word to him because she could not, her throat being so choked with anger, but in her heart she told herself that she would not rest by day or night until she had made him pay dearly for trading away the ewes.

When the king's son tried to tell her what exceptional qualities the hounds possessed, she would not listen to a word he said. She clapped her hands to her ears, and ran away from him into the wood and there he could not find her. He searched high, and he searched low, but never a sight or a sound of her did he get, so at last he went back to the shieling and there were his three hounds lying before the door.

"She's gone," he told them. And Luathas sighed, and Gramalas sighed, but Fios, to his surprise, spoke up and answered him. "Let her gang her ain gait!" said Fios, the wise one.

"Och, aye," answered the king's son. "So I will. Happen when her anger wears out she'll come running home again."

"Then—or before!" growled Fios.

So the king's fair son waited, and days came and went, one day after another, but his sister did not come back.

When the king's dark daughter ran away from her brother into the wood she did not stop and hide there, but ran straight through, and up the hill and down the other side. Anger gave such speed to her feet that she had run through seven shires, across three kingdoms, and over two mountains, fording all the streams on the way, before she stopped to rest. She sat on a bank by the side of the road and looked about her. Behind her was the mountain she had just run over, and before her a *baile-beag,* or small village of a dozen crofts or so, and on her right were the high steep crags above the sea. But over the moor to the left, and along way off, stood a great black castle upon a low rocky hill.

Some folk were coming along the road to the baile-beag, so the king's daughter stopped them, and asked, "Who dwells in yon black castle across the moor?"

At first they made no reply, but looked at her silently and uneasily, as if fear had made them dumb, but at last one of them said, " 'Tis the castle of the *Famhair,* the wickedest of wicked giants. His throat and his gullet are made of iron, and he holds in his mouth a great burning coal to keep his blood warm. His breath is so hot that one puff of it will burn to ashes anything that he blows upon."

"Famhair or not," said the king's dark daughter, "a castle is the right place for the daughter of a king and to the castle I'll go." And she got up from the bank upon which she had been sitting and off to the castle she went, while the villagers stood in the road, gaping after her. They shook their heads and said to one another, "Och, the lass is daft! That will be the end of her!" and then they went on their way.

But she had no mind to be burned up by the hot

breath of the Famhair. How she did it, no one knows, whether with fair words or foul words; whether with wiles and threats; some way, however it was, she got on the good side of the giant, and soon he was in her power and anything she asked him to do, he was willing to do. There are some who say that she was a witch and won him over with sorceries and spells. But, as the old wives' saying goes, like runs to like, and both of them being wicked, they made a fine pair. The two of them put their wits together, the Famhair and the king's daughter, and hatched a plot against her brother to punish him for trading off the ewes.

As for the king's son, there he was at the shieling, biding there until his sister came back again. Each morning he went out hunting with the three hounds, Fios, Luathas, and Gramalas, and each evening he returned to the little house, hoping to find his sister there.

"She will return only to harm you," warned Fios, the wise one.

"I cannot believe that," the king's son said. "But harm me or not, she is the child of my mother and the daughter of my father. She is my own sister, and I cannot forsake her. I shall bide here lest she come."

Luathas sighed and Gramalas sniffed, and Fios said no more. But one day when they returned from hunting, Fios stopped the king's son as they came through the wood.

"Your sister has come back," said Fios, the wise one.

"Let us hurry then to give her fàilte, and welcome

her home," said the king's son eagerly, hurrying his steps. But Luathas on one side and Gramalas on the other, and Fios before him, set themselves against him and held him back.

"Hear me now!" said Fios, the wise one. "She has brought with her the Famhair, a giant whose evil has few equals in this world. He and your sister have laid a trap for you to bring about your death."

"She would not do so!" cried the king's son. "She is my sister."

"She has done so already," said Fios. "Over the top of the door they have laid a dagger, double-edged and keen, and they have left the door a wee bit open, so that anyone who wishes to enter, when he opens the door wider, will dislodge the knife. Then the knife will fall upon him and pierce him to death. And if the knife should fail to kill you, the giant has dug a hole in the floor of the shieling where he and your sister are hiding, and if you escape from the knife with your life, the giant will burn you to death with his fiery breath."

But the king's son refused to believe the dog, forgetting that the crofter had told him that Fios had knowledge of everything in the world.

"Well, then," said Fios, the wise one. "Let Luathas go first and run through the house. Then you will see with your own eyes if I have lied to you or not." And to that the king's son agreed.

When they came out of the wood there was the shieling with the door ajar as Fios had said it would be. Fios and Gramalas stood with the king's son at the edge of the clearing while Luathas, the swift one, gathering himself together for flight, dashed through the house, knocking the door wide open as he passed. As the door flew open, from the lintel above it a sharp-edged dagger dropped and stuck quivering in the middle of the threshold. So swiftly did Luathas run that all the harm the dagger did to him was to clip off the ends of the last three hairs of his tail. Racing in one door and out the other, so fast that the eye could not follow him, Luathas was back with his companions before the knife had stopped quivering in the sill. But the wind of his passing was so great that it blew over the kettle that stood boiling on the hob, and the steaming water spilled out of it and scattered over the king's daughter and the giant in the hole where they were hiding, and scalded them both.

The giant, in pain and anger, began to scramble from the hole, swearing that he would have the lives of the king's son and his dogs, but Gramalas, the strong one, was watchful, and seeing that the Famhair was up to mischief, the big dog rushed up to the wall of the shieling and leaning his weight against it, brought the house down upon the giant's head. The heavy rafters and the stones from the walls came tumbling down upon the giant's head and shoulders, and the thatch of the roof half smothered him in its fall. The Famhair bellowed and roared and blew with rage and his fiery breath set fire to the thatch. The shieling blazed into flames and the Famhair and the wicked king's daughter were burned to ashes in the fire.

The king's son knew now that Fios had told him the truth about his sister, but still he grieved and wept for her after she was dead. He kept the nine days of mourning for her, fasting and praying for her sake. When the time of mourning was over, with his dogs beside him, the king's fair son turned away from the ashes of the shieling, and traveled over the roads of the world again.

They say that his dog Fios, the wise one, led the king's fair son to a distant kingdom where he was welcomed a thousand times over, and where the king was so pleased with him and his remarkable dogs that he would not be parted from them. The king gave the king's fair son his daughter for his wife, and half his kingdom beside. So all turned out well in the end for the king's fair son, but he always said that if the truth was to be known, he'd never have had a bit of luck in his life if he had not traded the three fat ewes for the three fine hounds, Fios, Luathas, and Gramalas.

The Ceabharnach

ONCE there was a man of Islay who had a very intelligent son. Even as a wee bairn he was so full of liveliness and mischief that the folk thereabouts took to calling him the Ceabharnach, that is, the Naughty Breeze, and the name suited him so well that soon few remembered that he had ever had another name. The father was not greatly blessed with the world's goods, but he saw that the lad had a very good mind, so he sent him to school and put him in the way of getting as much learning as he could afford. When the Ceabharnach came to the age of fourteen years, he told his father that he had learned all the schoolmaster could teach him, and a lot more that he had picked up here and there for himself.

"I've had enough of schooling," he said to his father. "And if there is any knowledge I lack, I can get it as I go along. You're wearing the life clean out of yourself fending for me. It's high time I was doing for myself."

So he got his father's blessing and bade him farewell till he came back again, and he promised that when he returned he'd have both their fortunes made.

It came into the mind of the Ceabharnach that he'd like to go to Erin, so he traveled along until he reached the sea, and there across the water the land of Erin lay. There was a garden not far from the sea in which there were trees upon which grew apples, so he plucked sixteen apples from the trees and went down to the shore. He threw one of the apples into the sea and set a foot upon it, then he threw another apple into the sea and set his other foot upon it. Then one by one, he threw the other apples into the sea before him, and set his feet upon them, one after the other, and when he stepped upon the sixteenth apple it brought him to Erin and he stepped off the apple onto the shore.

Then he went along the road, with his two elbows poking through the holes in his old coat sleeves; with his two ears poking through the holes in his old hat; with his square feet going clippety-cloppety, trippety-tattery in his old brogues with the cold ditch water running in and out of them; and with his old long sword sticking an ell's length out of a hole in the scabbard that hung crosswise at his backside. He went on until he came to the castle of the O'Donnell, and when he got there he took off in a great flying leap that lifted him over the walls, and over the towers, and brought him down in the middle of the courtyard where the O'Donnell was taking his ease.

"Och, wow!" cried the O'Donnell. "What in the world will that be, now?" He blinked his eyes twice and opened them thrice, and looked at the young lad standing before him.

"May the luck be easy on you, O'Donnell," said the lad.

"And to you the same," replied the O'Donnell. "And will you kindly tell me who are you and whence do you come?"

"I am the Ceabharnach," answered the lad. "I am master of all the arts, and I come from Scotland."

"Are you, now!" said the O'Donnell. "And what art can you be doing, then?"

"I can do harping," said the Ceabharnach.

" 'Tis the wrong place entirely that you've come to," said the O'Donnell. "For it's myself that has five-fifths of all the best harpers in Erin. Have I not Rory O'Calahan, and Tommy O'Gilligan, and Sean Cooney, as well as twelve others?"

Then the O'Donnell called his harpers to him and bade them all harp for the Ceabharnach to hear.

When they had finished, "Is that not harping?" the O'Donnell asked proudly.

"Well enough, if you like it," said the Ceabharnach.

89 .

"But on my way over to Erin from Scotland I passed by the Isle of Cats, and the miauling and caterwauling of the creatures there sounded better to my ears than the harping of your pipers here." And with those words the lad seized all the harps from the harpers, and breaking them up he made a fire of them, and stood over the fire warming his hands and feet at the blaze.

Then the O'Donnell was angry and leapt up to fight the Ceabharnach for losing him his harps. But the lad held him off, saying, "Peace, man! Do the harps mean so much to you?"

"I would give five marks for each of them, to have them whole and unburned!" the O'Donnell said.

" 'Twill be no harder to bring them back than it was to burn them," the Ceabharnach told him. "Put the marks in my hand, and you shall have your harps."

So the O'Donnell fetched a bag of money from his treasure room, and counted seventy-five marks, five for each harp, into the Ceabharnach's hand. The Ceabharnach stowed the money away in his sporran, then he took up a handful of ashes from the harps he had burned and rolled them and twisted them between his fingers, and they became a harp. And as good a harp it was, and even better, than the one he had burned. Then he did so again and again, until he had made harps for Rory O'Calahan, Tommy O'Gilligan, Sean Cooney, and the other twelve harpers as well, and put the harps into the harpers' hands.

But the harpers were angry because of the insult the Ceabharnach had put upon them when he compared their harping to the howling of the creatures on the Isle of Cats, so they all rushed at him to kill him. But he whipped his long old sword out of its scabbard and cut their heads off as they came at him, one by one.

"Ochone! Och, ochone!" lamented the O'Donnell. "Look at what you have done to me, O Ceabharnach! What shall I do for harpers now?"

"That you must answer for yourself," said the Ceabharnach. "I have tarried here long enough. I bid you good day."

And off he went, leaving the O'Donnell behind him mourning for his dead harpers who lay neatly in a row with their bodies on one side and their heads on the other, at O'Donnell's feet.

The Ceabharnach went out of the castle and as he passed through the village below the wall, he met a fisherman with a half-empty creel of fish.

"Fáilte," said the Ceabharnach, giving an eye to the fish. "The luck is bad today?"

"Is it not always bad, today or any day?" answered the fisherman, showing his meager catch.

"In that case, would you like to be making your fortune?" the Ceabharnach asked.

"And why would I not?" the fisherman said.

"Well, then," said the Ceabharnach. "In the court of the castle of the O'Donnell there are fifteen men lying with their heads cut off. You shall go to the castle and put their heads back upon their bodies and bring them to life again. But before you do it, demand a peck of gold and a peck of silver from the O'Donnell for doing the deed, and until you get it do nothing at all."

"Glory be to heaven!" the fisherman exclaimed. "I will do as you say. But how will I bring them alive again after their heads are on?"

"Pluck yourself a bunch of grass from the kirkyard," said the Ceabharnach. "When their heads and bodies are together again, dip the grass in water and sprinkle the lot of them well. They'll leap up in a trice, as well and strong as ever they were."

The fisherman got a bunch of grass from the kirkyard and rushed off to the castle of the O'Donnell, who gladly paid him the peck of gold and the peck of silver for which he asked. The fisherman did as the Ceabharnach had told him to do, and brought the fifteen harpers back to life again. Then all was joy in the castle of the O'Donnell, for the O'Donnell had his harpers and the fisherman's fortune was made.

The Ceabharnach went along the road again with his two elbows poking through the holes in his old coat sleeves; with his two ears poking through the holes in his old hat; with his square feet going clippety-cloppety, trippety-tattery in his old brogues with the cold ditch water running in and out of them; and with his old long sword sticking an ell's length out of a hole in the scabbard that hung crosswise at his backside. And he came to the house of Sean Mor Eilean and knocked boldly at the door.

"Who knocks at my door to open it?" Sean Mor Eilean called out. "Come into the house, for no man

stands on my doorstep who is not bidden to enter."
So the lad went into the house.

"Blessed be the day to you, Sean Mor Eilean," said
the Ceabharnach.

"And to you the same," returned Sean Mor Eilean.
"Who are you, and whence do you come?"

"I am the Ceabharnach, and I am master of all the
arts, and I have come to Erin from Scotland," the
Ceabharnach told him.

"What arts can you be doing then, O Ceabharnach?"
asked Sean Mor Eilean.

"I can do a juggle," the Ceabharnach said.

"You have come to the wrong house entirely," said
Sean Mor Eilean. "I have five-fifths of the best jugglers
in Erin, for I have Coltan O'Ballachan, and I have Tighe
O'Kelly, and better jugglers than those two never drew
mortal breath."

"We have better in Scotland," the Ceabharnach said.

"Let me see you do a juggle then," said Sean Mor
Eilean.

The Ceabharnach took three straws and threw them
into the air, and blew upon them to send them high,
then caught them upon the back of his hand as they
fell. Then he made his hand into a fist and blew the
straws off again.

"Hah!" laughed Tighe O'Kelly. "That is a juggle for
babes to do. I can do the like myself."

Then Tighe threw the straws up in the air and caught
them, and made his hand into a fist. But when he blew

upon the straws, his fist blew off with the straws, and there he stood, surprised and dismayed, with only one hand left.

"I will do another juggle," said the Ceabharnach, not waiting to be asked. He took hold of one of his ears and pulled it until he touched it to his nose, and when he let it go again, his ear sprang back into place.

"I can do that same juggle," said Coltan O'Ballachan. "Any fool could do the like." And Coltan took hold of his own ear, but he pulled at his ear so hard that his head came off, and there stood Coltan O'Ballachan, holding his head in his hand by his ear, and his head clean off his shoulders and a surprised look on his face.

Sean Mor Eilean looked at his two jugglers, one without a hand and the other without a head. "I'll grant that you have won with the juggling this day, O Ceabharnach," he said sadly.

"I have so," said the Ceabharnach. "Well, having bested both your men who are five-fifths of all the best jugglers in Erin, I see no need for staying with you any longer, so I'll be on my way."

"Och, nay! Nay!" cried Sean Mor Eilean. "You'll not be leaving my men in such a sorry state. Will you not mend them before you go?"

"I haven't the time to spare for it today," the Ceabharnach said. "Happen I'll be coming this way in another twelvemonth or so, and if I do I'll stop by and mend them, but if I do not you will have to keep them as they are."

Then the Ceabharnach walked out of the great house

of Sean Mor Eilean and left him sorrowing over his jugglers there.

The Ceabharnach went through the village that lay beyond the great house, and when he got to the end of it he met a farmer with a sack over his shoulder, and it no more than half full.

"Fáilte," said the Ceabharnach. "What is it that you have there?"

"A bushel of corn," said the farmer. "And it is the whole of my harvest for this year. The times are bad for the crops."

"Would you like to be making your fortune?" the Ceabharnach asked.

"Och, aye!" said the farmer. "And who would not?"

"In the great house of Sean Mor Eilean are his two jugglers, one without a hand and the other without a head, and himself sitting sorrowing beside them. If you mend them for him he will make you a rich man for the rest of your life."

"I'd not mind being rich at all," said the farmer. "But how can men in such a state be mended, I'd like to know?"

"Pluck a tuft of grass from the kirkyard," said the Ceabharnach, "and carry it up to the great house with you. When you get to the house strike a bargain with Sean Mor Eilean for a peck of gold and a peck of silver to mend his men, and make them whole again. When you have the money safe in your sack, put the head on the shoulders of the man who lacks it, and the hand on the wrist of the man who has but one hand.

Dip the kirkyard grass into water and sprinkle the two of the men with the water. As soon as you do that both of the men will be as well as ever they were."

The farmer ran off to the great house of Sean Mor Eilean with the bunch of grass in his sack. He made a bargain with Sean Mor Eilean for a peck of gold and a peck of silver, and when the money was safe in his sack, the farmer did as the Ceabharnach had told him to do, and mended Sean Mor Eilean's men. Then everybody was happy in the great house of Sean Mor Eilean, because Sean Mor Eilean had his jugglers again and the farmer had made his fortune and was a rich man for life.

So the Ceabharnach went along the road again with his two elbows poking through the holes in his old coat sleeves; and his two ears poking through the holes in his old hat; with his square feet going clippety-cloppety, trippety-tattery in his old brogues with the cold ditch water running in and out of them; with his old long sword sticking an ell's length out of a hole in the scabbard that hung crosswise at his backside.

Then he came to the kingdom of the king of Leinster, and he met the king and his huntsmen and his nobles riding out of the castle, going to the chase. The Ceabharnach stood in the road so that the king could not go by, neither to the left of him nor to the right of him, so the king and his party stopped.

"Fáilte, King of the Kingdom of Leinster," said the Ceabharnach. "May the hunting go well for you this day!"

"To you the blessing of luck, also," said the king. "Who are you, and whence do you come?"

"I am the Ceabharnach," said the lad. "I am a master of all the arts and I come from Scotland."

"What art will you be doing now?" asked the king.

"I will be at the art of hunting," the Ceabharnach said.

"Hunting?" exclaimed the king. "What would your age be, lad?"

"I am fourteen years of age, and soon will be fifteen," said the Ceabharnach.

"You must bide a few years," the king said, laughing. "You are not yet man enough to go hunting with me."

"If I do a man's share, will you give me a man's honors?" asked the Ceabharnach.

The king of Leinster liked the lad's spirit. He stopped laughing and had another look at the Ceabharnach. "Och, well, you might as well come along," said he. "And you'll be given whatever you earn." Then he turned to his huntsmen and bade one of them find the lad a horse.

"I have no need of a horse," said the Ceabharnach. "I will run with you on my two feet, and there will be no horse here today which will outrun me."

All day the king of Leinster and his men hunted, and the Ceabharnach hunted with them, and no horse outran him in the chase. But when the day was nearly over they had not yet brought down one stag. Fast before them the drove raced and twisted and turned, and the king and his men could not take so much as one deer of them all.

Then the king of Leinster wiped the sweat from his brow and cried out, "The curse of the devil is on this day and the hunting! We'll do as well to give it up and ride home."

The Ceabharnach, who was running beside the horse of the king, looked up at him and said, "I have a mind to show you the art of hunting. If I catch the drove and turn it to you, will you give me half of the value in gold of all the spoil you take?"

"That I will, O Ceabharnach," answered the king of Leinster. "Not only the half of the worth of the hunt will I give you, but my daughter to you in marriage, as well."

Then the Ceabharnach cut himself a whistle from the twig of a tree nearby, and told the king to bid his huntsmen stretch out their line to catch the deer as he drove them toward them. The Ceabharnach ran toward the drove and the deer took flight, but if they ran fast, the Ceabharnach ran faster, for he could catch the wind, but the wind could not catch him. He outran the deer, and getting before them, blew his whistle, and at the sound of the whistle the drove turned, and the Ceabharnach herded them all like kyne into the hands of the king and his men, and many a deer was slain in that day's hunting.

The king of Leinster was a man of his word. He gave the Ceabharnach a man's full honors for his share of the hunt, and of gold he gave half the worth of the great spoil that was won that day in the hunting, as he had promised to do. Then the king gave orders that prep-

arations should be made for the wedding of his daughter
to the Ceabharnach, which was to take place in two
days' time.

On the morning of the wedding day, while the bride
was being dressed and guests were riding in from all
directions, the Ceabharnach put his gold, and the
seventy-five marks he had got from the O'Donnell, into
a sack and took the sack upon his shoulder and out of
the castle he ran. Somebody caught sight of him and
gave the alarm, and all came running after, the king,
the queen, the nobles, the bride, and the guests and all.
They chased him all the way down to the sea, but they
never caught him, and how could they, if the wind itself
could never catch him?

There was a boat there by the shore, and he got into
it, and pushed away from the shore. Then he shouted out
to those who came after him, "Somebody else may marry
the daughter of the king of Leinster this day, but it
will not be me!" With that, he picked up the oars and
tore the sea to pieces in his haste to get back to the land
of Scotland on the other side.

When he got across the water, he landed on the shore
of Islay, and, taking his sack of gold upon his shoulder,
he started off for home. He went along the road with
his two elbows poking through the holes in his old coat,
with his two ears poking through the holes in his old
hat, with his square feet going clippety-cloppety, trippety-tattery in his old brogues with the cold ditch water
running in and out of them, and with his old long sword

sticking an ell's length out of a hole in the scabbard that hung crosswise at his backside, and he never stopped until he was under his father's roof once more.

Then to his father he said, "I have walked the roads of Erin from the castle of the O'Donnell to the kingdom of the king of Leinster, and I have made the fortunes of a fisherman and a farmer, and I have made yours and mine!"

"Did you now!" said his father. "Och, well, everybody has always said that I had a very intelligent son."

So the Ceabharnach and his father lived very merrily at ease on the Isle of Islay all the rest of their days.

The White Sword of Light

THERE was once a gruagach, a giant-woman this one was, who came over from Jura and went ravaging up and down among the islands. She was known as the *Gruagach-an-cas-fionna-donn* (the brown curly-furred giantess) because from head to toe she was covered with thick brown curly hair. Because of her horrible appearance and her wicked actions, she was the terror of the countryside for miles and miles around.

This monstrous creature came to a kingdom where a young king dwelt with his sister. She seized upon his castle and the young king she threw into his own dungeon, making him a prisoner there. His bonnie young sister she put in the castle kitchen and made her toil for her bread among the scullery maids, and then she took over the kingdom and ruled it to suit herself, and her rule was a hard one, as you may well believe.

There was a prince in a neighboring kingdom, a strong, handsome young fellow who had no fear of any man or beast that ever drew breath. He was the only son of his old father, who doted upon him and gave him a fine castle for himself and a bit of the kingdom to rule. Much as the old father loved his son, he knew he was inclined to be rash and headstrong, so he took the precaution of sending a wise man to dwell with the young prince, to guide him and give him counsel and keep him out of trouble as well as he could. The wise man did his best, and nobody could have done better, and times the young prince would heed his wise man's advice, but to tell the truth, more often he'd not.

The prince had a great passion for gambling and was exceedingly skillful at every sort of game of chance. The trouble was that he was so good at gaming that he had beaten all the best players in his father's kingdom as well as in his own, and he could find no one else worth spending his time upon. Then one day it came to his ears that there was a gruagach who dwelt in a castle in the next kingdom and she was a great one at all games of chance. The prince said to his wise man, "I have it in my mind that I'll be going this day to play a game against the Gruagach-an-cas-fionna-donn, the brown curly-furred one."

"Och, then you'll do better to put the thought out of

your mind," his wise man told him. "Not that you'll heed what I say," he added. "I might as well save my breath."

" 'Tis the truth you are telling," said the prince. "Whether you are for it or against it, I'm going just the same."

"Go, then," said the wise man. "Happen you'll be winning, and happen you'll not. But if you win, as well you may, when the gruagach asks what she must give you as a prize for your winning so that she may redeem herself, tell her that she must give you the young king whom she is holding prisoner in the dungeon of the castle."

"That I will do," said the prince, and off he went.

The prince came to the castle where the brown curly-furred giantess dwelt and challenged her to play a game with him. She was willing, so down they sat together and played. They played all day and they played all night, and it was the prince who won in the end.

"Och, the game is yours fairly," the gruagach said. "What will you ask of me as the price of your winning, that I may redeem myself?"

"You shall give me the young king whom you are holding prisoner in the dungeon below," said the prince.

The gruagach was not well pleased to give up the young king. She offered the prince money and treasures, all of which he refused. And, as he had won the game fairly, in the end she had to give him what he asked, so she had the young king brought up from the dungeon and gave him over into the prince's hands.

The prince took the young king home with him, and

then there was merrymaking. There was food in the place for feasting, and drink in the place for drinking; there was music in the place for singing and dancing, and everywhere there was rejoicing, because the young king was free from the gruagach, the brown curly-furred giantess.

When the time for merrymaking had passed, the prince said to his wise man, "It's in my mind that I'll go again to play a game against the Gruagach-an-cas-fionna-donn."

"You'll do better to put the thought out of your mind," his wise man told him, "and bide here at home, instead."

"I hear what you say but I'm not heeding it," said the prince.

"Go, then," said the wise man. "Happen you'll win again this time, and happen you'll not. But if you win, when the brown curly-furred one asks you what she must give you for your winning, tell her that you will take naught but the young king's sister who is in the kitchen of her castle among the scullery maids."

"That I will do," said the prince.

"Have a care," said the wise man. "The gruagach is wily and she will try to trick you. She will show you all the scullery maids and tell you that you may have the young king's sister if you can pick her out from the rest. That will be no easy task, for the lot of them will look as like to each other as peas, and with the smoke and grease from the kitchen that will cover them well, a body would never know which was the princess and which the serving lass. But watch carefully and you will see a wee black spider letting itself down from the rafters on a thread from its web. It will hang over the head of one of the lasses, and that is the one for you to be choosing, for she will be no other than the young king's sister."

"That I will do!" the prince said.

The prince came to the castle where the brown curly-furred giantess dwelt, and again he challenged her to play a game with him. She was willing, so they sat down and played. They played for two days and they played for two nights and in the end the prince won again.

"You've won fairly," the gruagach said. "What will you be asking from me for winning, that I may redeem myself again?"

"Give me the young king's sister that's down in the kitchen with the scullery maids," said the prince.

The gruagach was no more pleased with the forfeit he asked of her this time than she had been the other, but nothing she offered instead caused the prince to change his mind. In the end, since he had won fairly, there was naught she could do but consent. But since she could not persuade him to give up his prize, she did as the wise man had said she would, and tried to trick the prince.

"Och, then, 'tis fair awkward," said she. "There's a sluagh of scullery maids in the kitchen, and which would be the young king's sister I'd not be knowing myself. I'll tell you what—you shall have a look at them all yourself, and if you are able to pick the lass you want from among them, you may take her along with you, and welcome to her you'll be!"

The gruagach took the prince down to the kitchen and there they found scullery maids galore rushing about and toiling under the eye of the cook. The gruagach called the lasses together and stood them in a row. The prince walked up and down before them, looking them over as he passed slowly by. It was the truth his wise man had told him, for they all looked the same to his eyes, and they were so smeared and bedaubed with kitchen soot and grease that a body would never know what they were like under all the grime. Then a wee black spider dropped from the rafters and hung on a thread it had spun, swinging above the head of a lass in the middle of the row. The prince stepped up and took the hand of the lass. "This is the young king's sister," he said. "And now I'll be taking her home with me." The gruagach was mad with rage but she could not stop him, for he had won the game fairly, and named his forfeit to which she had agreed.

The prince took the young king's sister home to his own castle, and there he put her into the hands of the ladies of his court. They washed the soot and grease away from her, and they dressed her hair, and clad her in clothes that were seemly for the sister of a king. Then they brought her to the prince and when he laid eyes upon her, he discovered that she was so bonnie it took his breath away. He made up his mind to wed her if she would consent to have him, so he went to the young king and asked him for his sister's hand. The young king was willing and so was his sister, and for once the wise man was pleased with the prince, so he was willing, too.

Then there was a grand wedding with food in the place for feasting, and drink in the place for drinking. There was music in the place for singing and dancing, and there was great rejoicing because the prince had found himself a bonnie bride.

The wedding lasted for a year and a day, and when it was over the prince said to his wise man, "It's in my mind to go again to play a game against the Gruagach-an-cas-fionna-donn."

"You'd best bide here," his wise man told him. "For if you go I have my doubts that you will win this time. When you lose the gruagach will put trouble upon you and it will be many a long day before you come home again—if you ever do."

"Trouble or no trouble," the prince said, "I shall go just the same."

"Go, then," said his wise man. "But I will give you a spell to put upon the gruagach, so that if you lose she will do no mischief while you are gone. Heed me well, now, and do as I say. You must lay the spell upon the gruagach the minute she names the forfeit she wants, before she can open her lips to speak again. The spell will have no power over her otherwise."

"That I will do," said the prince. "Give me the spell and I'll be on my way."

The prince came to the castle where the brown curly-furred giantess dwelt and challenged her to play a game against him. She was willing, so they sat down and played. They played for three nights and three days, not stopping for bite nor sup. And in the end, it was the Gruagach-an-cas-fionna-donn, the brown curly-furred one, that won.

"You've won fairly," the prince said. "What forfeit do you ask of me for the winning, that I may redeem myself again?"

"Fetch me the Claidheamh-geal-solus, the White Sword of Light, that belongs to my sister the gruagach of Jura!" said she.

The prince was waiting for the last word to fall from her lips, and the moment it did he spoke up and laid upon her the spell his wise man had given him, before she could open her lips to say another word.

"I lay it upon you by spells and by crosses," said the prince. "That you shall stand upon the top of the top-most tower of this castle, and the heat of the sun shall beat upon you; the winds of the four corners of the earth shall blow upon you; the rains and the snows of the heavens shall fall upon you; and you shall not be able to shift a foot from the place where you stand until I return and give you leave to come down!"

Up to the top of the topmost tower of the castle the gruagach climbed, and there she stood. The spell of the wise man was much more powerful than any spell of her own, and she was compelled to obey it, not being able to help herself. The prince waited only long enough to make sure that the wise man's spell held the gruagach fast on the top of the tower, and then he turned his back to the castle and started off on his journey to fetch the Claidheamh-geal-solus, the White Sword of Light.

He traveled over mountain, he traveled over moor, he forded burn and river. He traveled by day and he traveled by night, and he came at last to the shore of the sea. There he found a boat, and stepping into it, he turned its stern to the shore and its prow toward Jura, and sailed away.

When he came near Jura he saw the gruagach of that island standing on a cliff above the shore, holding a magic ball of yarn in her hand. It was the custom of the giantess of Jura to stand there by the sea, and whenever a sailor came by in his boat she would hold the loose end of the yarn in her hand and cast out the magic ball, which would unwind until it reached the boat. Then the ball would fall into the boat and stick fast there, and the gruagach would draw the vessel in to the shore by the thread she held in her hand. Sailors whom she caught in this manner were never seen again.

When the giantess of Jura saw the boat of the prince she cast her magic ball out into his boat and drew it in to the shore.

"What fishie have I caught on my line?" cried the gruagach of Jura. "Och, now, 'tis a wee mannie! And what have you come here for, my bonnie wee man?"

The prince jumped out of the boat and faced the giantess boldly. "Thank you kindly for your help in bringing my boat in," said he. "But I'd have made out well enough without it. I've come from your sister, the Gruagach-an-cas-fionna-donn, the brown curly-furred one, who has bidden me to get from you the Claidheamh-geal-solus, the White Sword of Light, and fetch it back to her."

"My sister will wait many a long day before she gets it!" said the giantess with a great screech of laughter.

"She will wait no longer than it takes me to lay my hands upon it and carry it back," said the prince.

The gruagach was so pleased with the boldness of him, and with his handsome looks, that she took a terrible fancy to him, and it came into her mind that she'd like to keep him with her forever to entertain her and keep her company.

"I'll make a bargain with you," she said to the prince. "Stay here in friendship for a year and a day, and when the time is up you shall have the Claidheamh-geal-solus, the White Sword of Light, to take home with you. I'll give it to you myself."

The prince did not like the terms the giantess made, but when he found that he could not get better ones from her, he agreed. So he stayed with the giantess and kept her company, singing songs to her and telling her tales, to her heart's content, for a year and a day.

Many a time he thought of trying to get away from the gruagach, to seek out the sword for himself, but she gave him no opportunity. During his waking hours she was always at his elbow, and when he went to bed at night, he slept the sleep of the dead. His slumbers were so sound because, unbeknownst to him, the gruagach put a sleeping potion into the cup of wine she gave him at bedtime each night.

The year and the day went by at last, and the prince demanded that the gruagach keep her part of the bargain as he had kept his.

"Give me the Claidheamh-geal-solus, the White Sword of Light," said he, "and let me go on my way."

The gruagach burst into a sorrowful lament at his words. "Ochone," she lamented. "Och, ochone. Och, ochone.

"Och, then, little man of my heart, will you leave me?
Who, now, will keep me company?
Who, now, will sing me songs in the bright days?
Who, now, will tell me tales in the long nights?
Och, then, little man, will you go away from me?"

But the heart of the prince was not touched, for he knew that she was a creature of evil and deceit, and he did not trust her.

"I have stayed overlong as it is," he said. "I will stay no longer. Give me the sword!"

"Wait you here, then," she told him. "I will go fetch it for you."

She went, then, and took from among her weapons an old rusty sword upon which she laid a spell so that it shone like the high summer sun. She carried the sword back to the prince and when he saw its shimmering brightness he thought it was indeed the White Sword of Light. The prince took the weapon from the hand of the gruagach of Jura, and going down to the sea he got into his boat and set forth upon his journey home. The gruagach stood on the cliff above the sea and watched him go. When he had sailed out a distance from the shore, she cast the magic ball into his boat and began to draw it back to her. The prince drew the sword she had given him, to cut the thread, for he knew that the magic of the Claidheamh-geal-solus, the White Sword of Light, would be far greater than that of the ball of yarn. But the spell had left the sword, and the prince saw that it was naught but an old rusty blade which could not cut the magic thread.

The gruagach of Jura drew the boat up upon the sands, and the prince jumped out and threw the rusty sword at the feet of the giantess.

"Take back your false sword," he said angrily, "and give me the true one according to the promise you made."

"Och, my wee mannie," the giantess said. "I could not bear to be parted from you. When I bargained with you for a year and a day, I had not thought the time would pass so soon. Come, let us make another bargain. Keep me company here for another year, and you shall have the true Claidheamh-geal-solus at the end of the time."

But the prince would make no bargain with the giantess of Jura. She had tricked him once and he mistrusted that she would trick him again. "I'll take no promise from you and I'll make no bargains," he said. "I will stay, if I must, but no longer than the minute the White Sword of Light is in my hand, and I in my boat and on my way back to my own land."

But the prince had no more chance to seek the sword

than he had had before, for by day, there she was at his elbow again, and by night he slept too sound, never waking at all until morn, because the gruagach, as she had done before, was putting the sleeping potion into his wine.

For a fortnight or two, the prince fumed and fretted, and he began to wonder if it was to be his fate to remain with the giantess all the rest of his life. Then one night, as the giantess poured the wine for their evening draughts, he caught her dropping the sleeping potion into his cup when she thought he was not watching.

"Aha!" said the prince to himself. "So that is what makes me sleep so sound." But he gave no sign that he knew what she had done. She brought the two cups to the end of the table and set one in his place and one at her own. Then, as was her custom, she went over to mend the fire. The minute her back was turned, the prince switched the cups, putting his, with the sleeping potion in it, at the gruagach's place and taking hers for himself. When she came back, the prince was lying over the table with his head on his arms, snoring loud enough to wake the dead. There was no way she could know that he was only pretending to be asleep. Satisfied, she picked up the cup at her own place and drank the wine down at one gulp. It was not long before she herself was the one who was snoring, but there was no pretense about her slumber, for she was sound asleep.

As for the prince, he thought that he had never been wider awake in his life. Up he got, and began to go from room to room of the castle, searching for the White Sword of Light. He search high and he searched low and did not find it, while the night wore away and he despaired of finding it at all. Then just before daybreak, in a corner at the top of the castle, he found a wee room tucked away under the roof, with nothing in it but a tall wooden press. He opened the door of the press and a burst of light came out of it that made the room bright as day, and the heart of the prince leaped for joy, because he knew that he had found the Claidheamh-geal-solus, the White Sword of Light, at last.

The prince seized the sword and sped down the stairs and out of the castle, and down toward the shore, but before he had reached his boat, the day dawned, and the cocks crowed to greet the morn. The gruagach of Jura heard them and woke from her slumber, and looking about her, she saw at once that the prince was gone, and in the distance she could hear the pounding of his feet as he ran down to the sea.

She leaped to her feet and saw him racing away from her, with the bright sword under his arm, so she took after him, and as she lumbered along she lamented,

"Och, then, little man of my heart, will you leave me?
Who, now, will keep me company?
Who, now, will sing me songs in the bright days?
Who, now, will tell me tales in the long nights?
Och, then, little man, will you go away from me?"

The prince paid her no heed and she ran after him, and each of her strides were as long as seven of his own, but she could not catch him for he ran like the wild March wind. Straight to the shore he raced with the White Sword of Light and jumped into his boat. When the gruagach of Jura reached the cliff he was well on his way out to sea.

Then the gruagach of Jura cast her magic ball into the prince's boat and began to pull it back to the land, tugging away on the thread with all her might. Quickly, the prince drew the bright sword from its scabbard, and cut the magic thread. When the thread she was tugging on was cut, it slackened suddenly, and the gruagach lost her balance and, with a great thud, she fell upon her back to the ground. The cliff shook and crumbled under her weight and she began to slip down toward the sea below. She dug her heels into the ground to hold herself back, but she was so heavy, and she moved with such speed, that she could not stop herself. Swiftly she slid across the shore and far beyond it into the sea, and drowned there. If you go to Jura they will show you the two great furrows her feet dug in the cliff as she slipped down.

When the giantess was dead the ball of yarn lost its magic and stuck no longer to the boat. It rolled about under the feet of the prince, and he picked it up and tossed it into the sea. There it floated about until the waves carried it to land and cast it upon the shore where the sea birds pecked it to pieces and used the bits of yarn to line their nests and make them soft.

The prince set the stern of his boat to Jura and the prow to the open sea and sailed away toward his home.

When he got to the shore of his own land, he beached the boat and taking the Claidheamh-geal-solus he started off on his travels again. He traveled by night and he traveled by day, he forded burn and river. He went over moor and he went over mountain, and at last he came to the castle at his journey's end. There on the top of the topmost tower of the castle he saw the Gruagach-an-cas-fionna-donn, the brown curly-furred giantess, still standing, waiting for his leave to come down. She was well-weathered, for the heat of the sun had beat upon her, the winds of the four corners of the earth had blown upon her, the rains and snows of the heavens had fallen upon her, and she had not been able to shift a foot from the place where she stood all the time he was away.

When she saw him she screeched and waved her arms at him, and the rags and tatters of her garments flew about her, and the prince thought she looked for all the world like a great hoodie crow, cawing and flapping its wings, with its feathers ruffled by the wind.

"Have you fetched the Claidheamh-geal-solus, the White Sword of Light?" she shrieked down at him.

"That I have!" said the prince, and he held the sword up for her to see. But when he held it up, he turned the sharp edge of the shining blade toward her, and a great white light flashed out of it into her eyes and blinded her, and all her evil and all her spells were turned back upon herself.

"You may come down now," shouted the prince.

And at his words, she toppled and fell from the top of

118.

the tower with a great crash to the ground, and there she lay dead.

The prince left her lying there and made his way to his own land. When he got home the joy caused by his return passed all bounds, for he had been gone so long they had given him up as dead. Then there was merry-making, and there was food in the place for feasting, and drink in the place for drinking. There was music in the place for singing and dancing, and there was great rejoicing because the prince had come home safe and well.

When the merrymaking was over, the young king went back to his own castle, to reign over his own kingdom once more. Then the wise man said to the prince, "You'll do well to bide at home, now."

"That I will do!" said the prince, taking the advice of his wise man at last. And so he did, for he had had his fill of gaming and roaming, as he could prove by the Claidheamh-geal-solus, the White Sword of Light, which hung in an honored place in his great castle hall. So the prince stayed at home with his bonnie wife, the young king's sister, in great contentment, all the rest of his days.

The Water-Bull of Benbecula

LONG ago, on the Isle of Benbecula, there lived an old tailor, and he was the finest teller of *sgeulachden,* or old stories, to be found in those parts. There was one queer tale he liked to tell that was told to him by his grandmother a long, long time ago when he was but a wee lad, running barefoot along the shore. It was about something that happened to the daughter of a family who were neighbors of his grandmother's family many years ago. She herself was a wee bit of a lass at the time, his grandmother told him, but she heard her elders talking about it then, and it impressed her so greatly that she remembered it all the rest of her life.

There were a man and his wife on Benbecula who lived on a fine little croft which lay quite a way inland, out of sight and sound of the sea. They had a growing family, but at the time there were six bairns, three lads and three lasses, and the eldest daughter was about sixteen years of age and a great help to her father and mother, being handy both indoors and out.

One day after the evening meal was over, the crofter and his wife sat on the bench by the door taking a bit of rest together after the toil of the day. It was that hour when the shadows begin to lengthen and darken but twilight has not yet fallen, and the day still has some time to run before dark. The crofter always held that this quiet unhurried eveningtide was their reward for a day's work well done. As a rule no one passed by, for their neighbors were few and only one or two lived beyond on the road, but this evening as the two of them sat there, side by side, they saw somebody coming toward them along the road that ran by the croft, and presently they made out the figure of an old cailleach, and she a stranger to them both. She was clad in a decent black gown made of some sort of woolen stuff, with a snowy white apron to protect it, and over her shoulders hung a bright red cloak. She wore a high white mutch on her head with a goffered frill about her face and a black silk ribbon making a band and strings for it. A doucer, tidier old body you could not hope to find. Although she was old she held her body erect, and her back was straight, with never a sign of a stoop to it, and the tread of her foot as she came quickly toward them was as firm and light as that of any young lass.

When she got up to them she stopped and gave them a civil greeting. "Fáilte! A blessing on the house and to the master and mistress of it, and to all that dwell within it," said she.

"Fáilte!" replied the crofter and his wife. "And to you the same." Then, it being her turn to speak, they held their peace.

The old cailleach wasted no time in telling them who she was and why she had come.

"Mistress MacAndrew is my name," said she. "Happen you've noticed the house I dwell in, on beyond the village on the shore. But if you have not, you can inquire of anybody in the village and they'll tell you who I am. I'm not one to beat about the bush when I have something to say, and I'll not do so now. I have been told that you have a young daughter who is modest, willing, and not afraid to work. I have need of such a lass to help me in my house. Will you hire your daughter to me, crofter?"

"Lads are the man's concern; what the lasses do is for the woman to say," the crofter answered, and nodded toward his wife. "Ask herself what she has to say about it."

The crofter's wife did not answer at once, for such a decision could not be lightly made. There's much to think about before a mother consents to let the first child leave home. She'd miss the lass's help, but then the next younger bairn was beginning to make herself useful and soon would be able to take the lass's work over. Then there was the matter of the money the lass would earn if she took the place with Mistress MacAndrew. They were not poor here at the croft, but neither were they rich, and there were five bairns other than the lass to bring up and give a bit of learning to. It wasn't that they'd be taking the lass's wages for their own use, but they could put what she made by for her, and it would make a tidy sum for a dowry when the time came for her to wed. All the time the crofter's wife was weighing the matter in her mind she kept her eyes on the old cailleach, sizing her up, and she liked what she saw. A decent-seeming body, and one who looked as if she were used to being respected. You could be sure that she'd be strict with a lass, thought the crofter's wife, but she would not be hard upon her. The lines and wrinkles in the face of the old cailleach had been put there by age and compassion and not by ill temper and pride.

The old cailleach did not press the crofter's wife for an answer, but stood silent, waiting patiently for her to make up her mind. At last the crofter's wife said, "Let the lassie decide for herself. If she is willing to go into your service, I'll have naught to say against it."

So they called the lass and put the matter up to her, and asked her what she wished to do.

The lass looked the old cailleach over just as her mother had done, and her thoughts were very much the same. She liked the old woman and felt she was a body who could be trusted, and one a lass need never fear.

"I'll come to you, Mistress, if you like," said the lass.

Then the amount of the lass's wages were settled upon, and it was decided that early on the next Monday morn the lass should come to Mistress MacAndrew's house. And so she did.

The house did not stand in the village itself, but some way beyond it. There were small fields around the house, belonging to the place, and the field at the side farthest from the village ended at the cliffs above the shore, and beyond the shore was the sea. If the house was no better than the one the lass had come from, it was certainly no worse. There was a but and a ben to it, and a loft above, and off from the front room there was a small nook, like a wee room built on at the side, just big enough for a box bed and a press, and this the lass was to have for her own.

Behind the house was a garden and the stable yard, where there was a shed with a run for the fowls and a stable with four stalls in it. One of the stalls was empty, but two of them were kept for the cows to bide in when the weather was bad, and in the fourth stall stood the sleek little horse that drew the plow and pulled Mistress MacAndrew's wee cart. Everything indoors and out was as tidy and trim as Mistress MacAndrew herself.

The lass was kept busy, but the work was not hard, and no more than she had done at home. There was a man to do the heavier work outside, and Mistress MacAndrew worked along with the lass, but with tending the hens, and milking the cows, and keeping up the garden, and all the household tasks, a body was never idle at the house on the shore.

At first it seemed strange to be living so close to the sea. When it was stormy, or when the tide came in, the rush and surge of the sea amongst the rocks and against the shore disturbed the lass quite a bit. The plunge and retreat of the waves, the constant tonn-tunn, tonn-tunn, seemed to beat on her ears as she lay in her bed at night, but after a while she got used to it and it troubled her no more.

Between Benbecula and the Island of North Uist there were about six miles of sands and rocks which could be traveled over on foot when the tide was low and crossed by boat when the tide was high. But it was very dangerous, not only because of unseen rocks and deep pools of rushing water, but because of the queer creatures who lurked there. When Mistress MacAndrew had need of something from the village and sent the lass to fetch it, the villagers told her dreadful stories of mermaids, of gruagachs, of nyxies, and the like, and of the terrible Each-uisge, or Water-horse, who could change his form from man to beast at will. Many an unwary man or woman, they told her, had met death at the hands of these creatures. One never knew where one would be with them, so wily they were. The lass listened and shuddered with horror. "Och, tell me no more about it!" she cried. "I've ne'er heard the like of it in all my life! Och, you're having me on!" she said. "I do not believe the half of what you say!"

When the lass had served Mistress MacAndrew for a fortnight or two the old cailleach called her one morning and told her that she was a good lass, and had done her work very well.

"It's in my mind to give you a bit of time for yourself," said her mistress. "Then you can go home to see your family if you like. After the midday meal on Saturday you may put your work away for the time, and leave for your father's croft. I'll not expect you back until the Monday morn, but be sure to get here early so as to get a good start on the week's work."

The lass could hardly wait for the end of the week, but when Saturday came, off she went, singing every step of the way because her heart was so light.

Her family ran out, overjoyed to see her so soon, and she had a grand time, taking her place among them as if she had never gone away. But she did not forget that she had given her promise to come back early to the house by the shore. Long before sunrise on Monday, she rose and dressed herself, and started off on the road to Mistress MacAndrew's house.

When she left her father's croft the morning mists still lay heavy on the ground. Where the road dipped into a hollow, as it did now and then, the fog was so thick that she could not see her hand before her face When she came to these places on her journey, she had to feel her way along to make sure that her feet did not stray from the road. The last of these pockets of fog lay where the road ran along by a stretch of bog, and when she reached this place she hardly more than crept by. She went so slowly that her feet made no

noise, which was why she heard a faint sound somewhere beyond in the mist. She stopped and listened,
waiting for the sound to come again, trying to make out
what it was she had heard. It came again, a low moaning,
more like a weary whimpering, and it came from somewhere deep in the bog at her right.

"Lord-a-mercy!" cried the lass. "Some poor body, poor
soul! or some beastie, has mired itself in the bog!"

Well, there was only one thing to do, and that was to
get the creature, whether man or beast, out if its trouble,
and since there was no one about to help her, she'd
have to do it herself. She tucked up the skirt of her
Sunday gown, and kilted her petticoats above her knees,
and stepped off the road, setting one foot carefully
before the other on the tufts of solid earth scattered
through the bog.

The mists were beginning to rise and although the
shapes of things were still vague, she had less trouble
picking her way. She splashed on, hopping from tussock
to tussock, trying to keep from slipping into the slimy
ooze between the tufts of grass. She had come almost
to the center of the bog before she found what she was
looking for. Some class of young beast it was, but what,
she could not tell, what with the mists above and the
mire and water growth below. Somehow or other the
creature must have wandered into the bog and, flounder-
ing about among the rushes and reeds, it had been snared
in the tangled roots and stems of the water vines and
bog lilies which now held it fast. She knelt beside the
creature and working carefully and patiently she freed

it from the matted growth about it, and as she pushed away the last twining stem, the sun shone out, clear and bright, and its rays came cutting through the mist. It was not until then that the lass was able to make out what the creature was.

"A bullock calf!" cried she. "*Och,* the poor wee beast!"

She drew it out of the mire onto a tussock not far from the one she knelt upon herself, and tried to stand it upon its legs, but it was too weak to keep its feet.

"My Sunday gown will be spoilt," she said with a sigh. "But there's naught I can do but pick you up, my wee bullock calf, and carry you myself."

And she gathered the beastie up into her strong young arms and carried it out of the bog, and down the road, and all the way to Mistress MacAndrew's stable, and there she laid it down in the empty stall.

The plowman and Mistress MacAndrew came running to see what the lass had brought. When the plowman came into the stable and laid his eyes on the bullock calf, he threw up his arms and screeched.

"'Tis a *tarbh-uisge,* a water-bull you've got there," he cried. "Turn him loose, or you'll rue it, for he belongs to the People of Peace, the fairy folk. Put him off the place as quick as you can!"

"Och, havers!" the lass said scornfully. "'Tis naught but a wee creature that got himself lost in the bog. 'Tis naught at all, man, but a wee bullock calf."

"No true bull ever looked like that one," the plowman insisted. "Look at the coat on him! Is it not gray as the sea water on a stormy day? And who e'er saw a crofter's bull with full-grown horns at that age, and those horns pointing the wrong way? I'm telling you, the creature's not canny, and you'll do well to rid yourself of him quick!"

"Hauld your whisht, man!" said Mistress MacAndrew. "The poor creature needs attention, and, tarbh-uisge or not, he'll be getting it, too. If the lass wants to keep the bull, then she shall, providing its rightful owner cannot be found. For that matter I never heard of a fairy creature doing anyone any harm when it was treated well. On the contrary, those who accommodate the fairy folk in their time of need, are always well rewarded in the end."

"Have it your own way," grumbled the man. But he would never go near the water-bull again.

"Now, lass," said Mistress MacAndrew. "The bull is yours, if no body comes to claim it, but if you keep it, you must take care of it yourself. And now the morn's well on and we're late. Get yourself out of your soiled clothing and into your work gown. We must make up for lost time." But if her words were sharp, her voice was not, and the lass knew that her mistress was not angry with her for holding back the day's work, and best of all, the wee bullock calf was her own.

No owner came to claim the bullock calf, so the lass took it into her care, and tended it well. She cleaned the deep cuts made by the tough stems of the water plants and dressed them with tar until they healed. She groomed him, brushing his curly gray coat each day until it was soft and glossy, and she polished his horns and his hoofs until they shone. He began to look for her each day, and when she came into the stall he'd paw the ground for joy and nuzzle his head against her arm as if he were an affectionate dog. He grew by leaps and bounds, it seemed, and soon was a great hulk of a beast, but to the lass he was always the wee bullock she found in the bog.

Mistress MacAndrew came now and then to have a look at the bull. "You've done well with him," she told the lass. "He's a grand big creature. He does well to love you. Did you not save his life?"

One day, after the bull was full grown, the lass went out to the field above the shore on the far side of the house. She carried a basket of linen to lay it to bleach on the grass. While she was spreading it out she looked up for a moment from her work and saw a man coming toward her up the cliff from the shore, swinging lightly and quickly along the steep path. He was a stranger, but that she would not have minded very much, but there was something about him that she did not like. She could not have put what she felt into words, but the way he looked at her gave her a terribly eerie feeling, and she did not like it at all. It made her so uneasy that she turned and sped back to the house and hurrying in she shut the door behind her and leaned against it, breathing hard.

"What's amiss!" asked Mistress MacAndrew sharply, looking up from her spinning wheel.

"There was a man came into the field where I was laying the linen," the lass said, "and he frightened me."

"You did well to come back to the house," said Mistress MacAndrew. She got up from her stool and went to look out the window. "Well, he is not there now," she said.

Two weeks later, or maybe three, the lass took a pail and a spud and went down the cliff to gather whelks from the shore. Soon she saw the same man again, coming along the sands. She dropped the spud and the pail, and left them behind her, and up the cliff she climbed as fast as she could go, but this time he followed after her. But before he could reach her the bull began to stamp and bellow in his stall, snorting and roaring with all his might. The man, hearing the bull, turned about and went back swiftly the way he had come.

The lass ran into the house. "Och, Mistress Mac-Andrew," she cried out. " 'Twas that man again."

Mistress MacAndrew looked troubled. "What in the world can he be wanting," she said, "that he does not come to the house like an honest man and state his business here?"

But when they went and looked out the window no man was in sight. All they saw was a great white horse, far away, walking along the shore at the water's edge.

"It was my good little bull from the bog that frightened the man away," the lass said.

"I do not doubt it," Mistress MacAndrew said. "Do you know, lassie, happen your bull is a tarbh-uisge, a water-bull, after all. How else would the creature have known you needed his help, since you did not call out and he could not see you from his stall in the barn?"

"Och, no," the lass said, laughing. "He's naught but my wee bullock calf that I got out of the bog."

Days went by, and weeks went by, with no sign of the stranger. The lass began to forget about him and went, untroubled, about her work. Then, one day when she was in the field above the shore, he came again. He stood at the edge of the field and spoke softly to her, and his voice was gentle and low. He made no move to come closer to her, so the lass, who had been thinking of running away, stopped and waited in the middle of the field. He was no longer a stranger to her, for she had seen him twice before, and as long as he kept his distance she was not afraid. Let him stir one step toward me, she told herself, and he shall see how I can run! But the man kept to the edge of the field where the path came up the cliff from the shore, and kept on talking to her all the time. She was curious, as all young lasses are, so she stood listening, because she wanted to hear what he had to say.

Then he wooed her with soft words, with sweet words, with words as gentle as the rustle of the sea breeze through new green leaves, with words that sounded like music to her ears. His voice so beguiled and charmed her that she forgot all her fears, and let him approach her and take her by the hand. He told her that he had journeyed from far-off places just to lay his eyes upon her bonnie face. He told her that he had come a great distance, drawn by his love for her. He said he was worn and weary with traveling, and begged her to sit down upon the soft grass and let him lay his head in her lap to rest, and maybe to sleep for a while. The sound of his voice and the words he said so enchanted her that she consented and sat down. Then he gave her a golden comb to comb his hair with, and laying his head in her lap, he fell asleep.

The lass sat, humming a quiet lullaby and combing his hair with the golden comb, and what with the warmth of the sun and the peaceful day, she was near to falling asleep herself. The comb slipped from her hand and when she caught it up the end of it caught the locks of his golden hair and parted them the length of his head. Then she saw at the roots of the hair there was white sand and seaweed of the sort that is never found but in the depths of the deep, deep sea. At once, the spell laid upon her by his voice held her no longer. The enchantment ended and she was terrified. She knew that this was no mortal man who lay sleeping with his head on her lap. It was the Each-uisge, the Water-horse, that the villagers had told her about. She saw her danger and understood very well that unless she could manage to escape from him, when he awoke he would carry her into the sea where she would drown.

There was only one thing that she could think of to help herself out of the fix she was in, and whether it would be of use she did not dare to hope very much, but she would try it anyway. With the comb in one hand, she went on combing his hair, but with the other hand she felt at her back and unfastened the strings of her apron and the waistband of her skirt. Working with great caution, she slipped off apron and skirt and got herself clear of them, then she laid his head very gently upon the garments she had shed. She sprang away then and, in her petticoats, she took to her heels and fled toward the house.

Almost at once he woke up, and finding her gone, leaped to his feet and came after her. She ran fast, but he ran faster, and although she had a good start to begin with, she knew, without turning her head to look, that he was gaining upon her all the time.

Then the bull in his stall screamed thrice, beating his hoofs upon the floor of the byre. The lass cried out to him and he answered, snorting and roaring and bellowing as if to bring the stable down. Mistress MacAndrew looked out to see what was amiss, and when she saw the lass flying toward the house with the strange man close behind her, she wasted no time. Out the back door she raced to the stable and let the bull out of his stall.

When the bull saw the man speeding after the lass he gave a great roar, fit to shake the earth, and rushed between the man and the lass. The lass darted into the house and dropped to the floor, half dead with terror, and there Mistress MacAndrew found her, and she with the golden comb still clasped in her hand, when the mistress came back from letting out the bull.

The bull whirled about upon the man, with his head lowered ready to gore him, but in a trice the man changed his form and became a great white steed. He was indeed the Each-uisge, the dreaded Water-horse. But the bull was beyond caring for that. Let the creature be what he might, the bull was truly a water-bull, and the mightiest one that ever came from the Sidhe, the People of Peace, and feared no beast in the world of fairy or man.

Then the two creatures, the great white steed and the great gray bull, rushed at each other and a grand battle began. They fought on the field, and they fought down the cliff, and they fought upon the shore. They fought amidst the rocks and the waves along the shore of the sea. They snorted and blustered and roared till the noise rumbled about the sky like thunder, and their hoofs struck the rocks with such force that sparks and flashes of fire sprang out. They stamped upon the waves until the waters of them turned into spray and mist and spume, and rose about them like a great fog, so that the two beasts in the middle of it could not be seen.

The villagers of Benbecula hid themselves in their houses, not knowing what to make of it all, and the folks on the Isle of North Uist, six miles away over the sea, thought that a terrible storm was going on over at Benbecula, and hoped it would not come their way.

The water-bull and the Water-horse fought up and they fought down, and in and out again, but in the end the water-bull won, and killed the Water-horse. Then the water-bull lifted the body of the Water-horse on his big strong horns, and with a great heave he tossed it far out to sea, where it sank and was never seen again.

Then the water-bull galloped away, with a grand flourish of horns and hoofs, and he went singing, over and over again:

> "The lassie of Benbecula,
> She saved my life for me,
> And I have saved the lassie's life,
> Now the tarbh-uisge is free!"

Mistress MacAndrew and the lass stood at the door, listening, and heard the song grow fainter and fainter, and farther and farther and farther away, until there was no more of it than a soft whispering of the words coming by on the wind, and then it was heard no more.

As they turned to go into the house, Mistress Mac-Andrew said, "Well, lassie, the plowman was right about it. Your beastie was a water-bull after all."

"Aye," said the lass. "Aye, my wee bulloch was a water-bull." But she turned her head away, so that Mistress MacAndrew should not see that she wept because he was gone.

After that day, there was no Water-horse to trouble the lass, so she laid out the linen in peace. But neither was there a water-bull in the stall in the stable, and the lass, for many a day, sorely missed her wee bull that she found in the bog. She stayed on with Mistress Mac-Andrew for several years after that, until a fine young man came along and asked her to be his wife. He was the sort of lad that any lass would be proud to take, so she consented and they were wed. She had for her dowry not only the wages she made while she was with Mistress MacAndrew, a tidy sum which her mother and her father had laid by for her, but she had also the golden comb that had been put into her hand by the Each-uisge, the Water-horse.

The Three Teeth of the King

Upon a fair summer's day a king went out to stroll about in the green meadow outside his castle wall. With him went all the company of his court, his nobles, his warriors, and his gentry, while his older son walked at his right hand and his younger son at his left.

Then one of the company who had more words than wits said to the king, "How could there be a safer place for Your Majesty than here in the midst of your warriors, with the great nobles and the gentry of the kingdom to protect you, so that no man in all the four corners of the world would have the daring to come and put insult or dishonor upon your royal head?"

"Is it daft that you are!" the king rebuked him. "Let me tell you, there is not a man on earth who can be wholly safe, even amidst his own folk. Why, a stranger might come and put shame upon me, even here, and be gone again so swiftly that none of you could so much as pluck a hair from his head!"

And so it was that it happened. There was the dark cloud of a summer storm rising from the west, and behind the cloud a horseman riding upon a black horse. Swiftly and easily the rider cantered up to the king, while his people, fearing the flying hoofs of the steed, made way on either side. Then the rider, making a fist of his hand, struck the king under his nose, and the blow knocked out three of the king's front teeth, which he spat out from his mouth. The stranger caught them as they fell and dropped them into his pouch, and then he turned his horse quickly, and riding away with great speed was soon hidden from them in the cloud of the storm.

"See, now!" said the king. "Was I not telling you that this could happen? All of you saw the affront put upon me, yet which one of you was able to touch even a hair of that dark stranger's head?"

Then his oldest son spoke up. "I lay it upon myself as *cain*," said he, "not to eat meat or drink more than once, in any one place, nor to tarry the length of a whole day in any one place, until I have cut off the fist that struck out my father's three teeth."

"I lay it upon myself, the same," said the second son,

"until I take off from his shoulders the head of the man that planned the offense."

There was one of the gentry standing beside the king's sons, and he was a man whose heart was filled with love and good will toward the king. His name was Mac-an-Coill'uaine, which is to say, the Son of the Green Wood, and he had served the king in battle well. "I lay upon myself the same cain!" cried he. "And I shall not stop to rest my feet nor to empty the sand from my shoes until I have cut out the heart from the man who struck the blow, and fetched the king's three teeth back to him again."

The king's two sons made a great jest of the words of Mac-an-Coill'uaine, and jeered at him for hoping to equal the deeds of princes of the royal blood. "You need not think you'll get leave to go along with us," said they. "A pitiful wretch, you'd run like a mouse when danger showed its face. It's likely you'd end up dead in a bog, or in a ditch by the side of the road, or fall over a crag before you'd traveled far. Great heroes spring from the race of kings!"

"Be that as it may," said Mac-an-Coill'uaine. "I'm going along."

The two sons of the king went along the road, and when they had gone some distance from the castle, the older son gave a look behind him, and there was Mac-an-Coill'uaine following in their tracks.

"What shall we do with that one?" the older son asked his brother.

"Cut his head off," the younger brother said.

"Och, we'd not be wanting to do that!" said the older brother. "But there's a good big crag to the side of the road ahead. We'll bind him tight to the great stones and he'll follow us no more."

So they waited for Mac-an-Coill'uaine, and when he came up to them they bound him with ropes to the great stones of the crag, and leaving him there, they went on their way.

They went another distance and the older king's son took a look behind him again, and there was Mac-an-Coill'uaine coming after, bearing the stones of the crag to which he was bound upon his back.

"There's that one coming behind us again, and the crag with him on his back," said the first king's son. "What shall be done with him now?"

"Cut off his head. Then he'll follow us no longer," said the second king's son.

"Nay, we'll not do so," said the first king's son. "Och, two great warriors like ourselves have no need to mind a poor creature like that, should he follow after us or not. Look now, brother, we have need of a ghillie to serve us, and keep our armor in order, and find us food to eat. Let us loosen the crag from his back and take him with us. We can travel free and easy with him to do the hard work."

And this they did, cutting the ropes and letting the stones fall from his back, that they might make him toil for them, while they traveled at their ease.

Not that day nor the next one, but toward the end

of the third day the two king's sons and Mac-an-Coill'-uaine came to the sea, and there at the shore they got themselves a ship to carry them farther. They set her stern to the shore and her prow to the sea and off they sailed, with her sails hoisted to catch the breeze to take them on their way. After three days of sailing the king's sons grew weary of the voyage, and said that one should go up the mast to see what could be seen from there.

"Och, you two are the great heroes," said Mac-an-Coill'uaine, "and I naught but the pitiful body who would lie dead in a peat bog or in a ditch by the side of the road. Let one of you go up the mast."

The first son, greatest of heroes, made a rush at the mast, to climb it, but before he was halfway up his courage failed him and he grew dizzy, and down he fell and lay in a faint on the deck.

"Well, they cannot say you did not try it," said Mac-an-Coill'uaine. "The pity is that your courage did not hold out."

"Leave it to me," said the second king's son, and he went up the mast, but halfway up his courage went the way of his brother's, and there he clung, neither able to go up nor come down, and Mac-an-Coill'uaine had to climb up and help him back to the deck again.

"Well, it was not for lack of trying," said Mac-an-Coill'uaine.

"Let you do it yourself!" the two king's sons told him.

"Aye, then," he answered. "And I but the pitiful body that would lie dead in a peat bog or in a ditch by the side of the road. But I will go up the mast for you,

143 .

and tell you what I see." So then he set the point of his spear and the points of his toes on the deck and gave a great leap, and up he went and landed in the crosstrees at the head of the mast.

"What do you see?" asked the first king's son.

"I see a black speck, and it too big for a bird and too small for land," Mac-an-Coill'uaine called down.

"Stay up there for a while," they told him, "until you see more."

So Mac-an-Coill'uaine stayed there at the top of the mast for a while, and then he gave a hail.

"What do you see?" they asked him.

"I see a big island," answered Mac-an-Coill'uaine. "And above the shore there is a ring of fire that goes all around the island, hemming in the land inside."

"Come down now," said the two king's sons. "And we will sail to the island."

So he came down and they sailed to the island. They went around it until they found the side where the wind was blowing the flames away from them, and there they got out of their ship and pulled it up on the shore. They sat down on the sands and looked at the ring of fire that leaped and flamed above the shore.

"One must go over the fire," said the first king's son.

"Och, you are the great heroes," said Mac-an-Coill'-uaine, "and myself naught but the pitiful body who would be lying dead in a peat bog or in a ditch by the side of the road. Let one of you go over the fire."

The king's sons looked at the fire with no great pleasure, but they were ashamed to be daunted with

Mac-an-Coill'uaine there to see. So the first king's son made a leap to pass over the fire, but he fell short, and all he got for his trouble was a good singeing from the fire, which sent him back to his companions in a hurry, and he would not try it again.

"Well, they cannot say you did not try," said Mac-an-Coill'uaine.

Then the second king's son tried it, but he fared worse than his brother, for he came down with one foot in the flames and limped back to the shore faster than he went the first time.

"If you did not make it, 'twas not for lack of trying," said Mac-an-Coill'uaine.

"Try it yourself!" the king's sons told him.

"That I will," said Mac-an-Coill'uaine. "But since I have no notion of what may lie on the other side of the fire, and what dangers may await for me there, you must trade your armor for mine, for yours is better by far." That they were only too willing to do, rather than try to leap over the fire again. So he chose the armor of the oldest king's son, because it was the best, and when he had dressed himself in it, he walked to the edge of the fire. He set the tip of his spear and the tips of his toes to the ground and made a great leap, and over the flames he went, and came down on the other side, well away from the fire. When he got there he looked around him, and saw nothing but bare ground with a stony hill rising above it a short distance beyond where he stood. So he went up the hill and looking down the other side of it he saw at the foot of the hill a little jewel of a woman, the bonniest he had ever seen, sitting there on the ground. There was a young man lying asleep with his head in her lap, and she was combing his hair.

"Do you belong to this place, my little jewel?" Mac-an-Coill'uaine asked.

"Not I," said she. "This is the son of MacDeorcha, the Son of Darkness, and his father stole me away from my father's kingdom seven long years ago. MacDeorcha has laid it upon me as spells and crosses that I must stay here on this island until I agree to wed his son, or until his son is dead."

"Wake him up, and he shall do battle with me," said Mac-an-Coill'uaine. "And if MacDeorcha's son is not dead at the end, then I myself shall be."

First he blew in the ear of the sleeping man, to wake him, but the man slept on. Then he pricked him with his spear, but the man did not so much as flutter an eyelid.

"You'll not wake him that way," said the little jewel. "He sleeps too sound. The only way you will wake him is to throw one of the big stones from the hill upon him."

So Mac-an-Coill'uaine reached down one of the great boulders from the crag of the hill above him and threw it with all his might, and the boulder hit the young man squarely in the middle of his chest. The young man opened his eyes then, and stretched himself and yawned, and looked about to see what had wakened him. When he saw Mac-an-Coill'uaine he leaped to his feet, drawing his sword, and rushed at him to kill him for making so free with him. Mac-an-Coill'uaine was ready for him, so the two of them went at each other, blow for blow. It was a notable battle, and in the struggle the two of them trod the hill down and trod it up again. They trod bog into dry land, and dry land into stones, but in the end Mac-an-Coill'uaine slew the son of MacDeorcha and cut off his head. Then he cut off the man's right hand, and cut the heart out of his breast. He looked into the young man's pouch and there he found three teeth and, being confused by the battle, he thought they were the three teeth of the king, but they were not, for they were only teeth from the jaw of an old horse instead.

He put the three teeth into his own pouch and then he said to the little jewel of a woman, "Now, my bonnie lass, you are free from the spells and crosses laid upon you, since the son of MacDeorcha is dead. Will you stay here on the island or will you go with me?"

"I had liefer go with you than with any man I have ever seen," the little jewel said.

So Mac-an-Coill'uaine strung the head and the hand and the heart of the son of MacDeorcha on a hazel twig, and taking the little jewel of a woman upon his back he leaped over the fire to the shore again. There he gave the hazel twig and the three teeth to the two king's sons to hold for him, and told them to wait there for him with the little jewel of a woman, while he went back over the fire to see what else he could see.

He went over the fire and climbed the hill again, and when he got to the top he looked back the way he had come. What did he see but the ship that had brought him to this place, with its sails spread, and already well out to sea, and it bearing the two king's sons and the little jewel of a woman away!

"A curse be on those traitors, the king's sons!" cried Mac-an-Coill'uaine. "They have stolen from me the spoils of my battle and my little jewel as well, and left me alone here to perish on this empty deserted isle."

Since there was nothing else he could do, he set forth to see what this strange place was like. When he had walked for a weary while and seen nothing worth laying his eyes upon, he came to another hill that rose from the stony wasteland. He climbed to the top and looked down upon a wide grassy plain, and at the edge of the plain a castle stood. So down the hill he went, and over the plain, and when he reached the castle he went in.

In the great hall of the castle there were three men who sat at a table by the fire. The men sprang to their feet when Mac-an-Coill'uaine entered and turned to face him so that he saw their faces plainly, and to his surprise he saw that they were his own three foster brothers who had disappeared from their own land half a dozen years or more before. They knew him at once and embraced him with joy and bade him welcome, but when he asked them how they had come to this island of fire, their eyes filled with tears of sorrow, and they told him that they had been captured while hunting and carried away from their country by MacDeorcha and his sons, who held them under a magic spell, and they had no hope of ever being free men again.

But why let their plight tarnish the joy of seeing

him again, said they, he being the first cause they'd had to rejoice in all the years they had spent in this place? So with food and drink they feasted, and passed the time with laughter and song, to celebrate his coming, and did not lay down to rest until the night was late.

In the morning Mac-an-Coill'uaine was wakened by a great clanging and clashing and opened his eyes to see what was afoot. There were his foster brothers dressing themselves in their armor and preparing for battle, in great haste.

"What is the reason for this?" he asked them, amazed.

"Och, 'tis part of the spell MacDeorcha, the Son of Darkness, has laid upon us," they told him. "Every morn at daybreak we must go out and do battle against him and his thirteen sons and one hundred of his men. We fight them all day until nightfall, and we leave them all dead on the plain, but in the twilight a gruagach, a horrible giantess who is the mother of MacDeorcha, comes and with a box of magic ointment she brings them all back to life again, so that we must meet them and battle with them all over again the next day. Only one day in seven we have to ourselves, for that day MacDeorcha goes out to do mischief in distant parts. That day was yesterday, which is why you did not find us at battle when you came, but it is our fate to go out to fight again this day."

"I will go out with you then and help you," said Mac-an-Coill'uaine, getting into his armor. "I'll promise you that when I am done with them they will not come alive again."

"That you cannot do," his foster brothers told him. "For by spells and crosses no man can come with us. When we go, we must go alone."

"If I cannot go with you, I shall go without you," said he. "No man has laid a spell upon me! Stay you at home and rest today, and I will go alone to fight."

So the three foster brothers remained at home while Mac-an-Coill'uaine went out to fight instead. There on the plain were MacDeorcha, Son of Darkness, and one hundred of his men, but there were only twelve of his sons with him that morning because Mac-an-Coill'uaine had slain the other one on the other side of the island before. When he laid his eyes on MacDeorcha he knew him to be the man who had come riding on his black horse behind the storm cloud to insult and shame the king by knocking out his three teeth. The blood of Mac-an-Coill'uaine boiled with anger as he remembered the dishonor done to the king, and his fury lent the strength of a hundred men to his arm. All day long the battle raged and when the sun set, with his last stroke he slew MacDeorcha and brought him down beside the dead bodies of his twelve sons and all his men.

Mac-an-Coill'uaine was fair spent by the fight, and torn and worn by the blows he had taken. He lay down beside the body of MacDeorcha to gather a bit of strength, for he was too weak to make his way back to the castle again. As he lay there in the gloaming he heard a great thump-thumping, and he lifted his head to see what made such a din. He saw the gruagach, the giantess who was the mother of MacDeorcha, coming his way with the box of magic ointment in her hand. No sight he had ever seen before in his lifetime was as horrible as what he saw now. The creature had twice the height of a tall man, her arms and legs were like trunks of trees, and her shoulders were the breadth of a door. Her face was lined with gullies like a hillside after a spring freshet, her mouth was as wide as a cave of the Cuilleans, and her front teeth which stuck out of her jaw were as long as the needles women make use of when they knit. She was clad from waist to feet in the trousers of a man, but above her waist the hair grew long and thick and brown and covered her, back and front, like a kilted plaid. She came up to Mac-an-Coill'uaine where he lay in the twilight, and dipping her finger in the magic ointment she bent over and groping about in the shadows she put her finger with the ointment on it into his mouth. Then Mac-an-Coill'uaine gripped his jaws together like an iron trap and bit her finger off.

"Ai-ee! Ai-ee!" the giantess screeched, and raised her foot to kick Mac-an-Coill'uaine, while she shook her hand with the pain. But the ointment she had put in his mouth had given him back his strength and made him stronger than before, so he leaped out of her way, and having left his own sword on the ground behind him, he snatched up the sword of MacDeorcha out of his dead hand as he passed by. The gruagach came after him with her own sword in her hand, and for a while they had it hot and heavy, with both of them laying on with a will. The gruagach had the heavier stroke, but like most giants, her sight was none of the best, and in the twilight she had a hard time keeping Mac-an-Coill'uaine under her eye. As for Mac-an-Coill'uaine, he was nimble and managed to keep out of the way of many of her blows, but, still and all, he was doing her little harm with his sword, while she was giving him plenty of trouble with hers. He doubted, the way the fight was going, whether he'd be able to hold out much longer.

Then the gruagach, thinking she felt him falter, laughed. "*Hiu! Huch!*" she chuckled. "You may as well give up, little man, for you'll never best me. I can only be killed by a blow above the belt of my trews, and you cannot reach so far."

Mac-an-Coill'uaine looked up to the waistband of the gruagach, and it was well out of his reach, as the creature said. But if he had not length in his arm, he had good wits in his head. "A blessing on you, O gruagach, Mother of MacDeorcha!" said he. "And it's myself is sorry you did not tell me that before!"

He began to fight harder than ever, giving three blows to the gruagach's one, but only one of them went the gruagach's way for the other two went to the ground behind him where he was digging a hole with the point of his sword. He had nearly reached the end of his strength by the time the hole was deep enough, but at last it was done. He gave one more cut to the legs of the giantess, and then he leaped backward and lit on his feet on the far side of the hole. The gruagach had not noticed what he was doing, and when he

jumped back she followed close after, thinking he meant
to run away. Down she came, into the pit that Mac-an-
Coill'uaine had dug with his sword. She landed with
such a thud that it made her teeth rattle, and she
shouted loud at the shock. It took her wits away for
to run away. Down she came, into the pit that Mac-an-
Coill'uaine was watchful, and there before his eyes,
and within easy reach of his weapon, was the waistband of the gruagach's trews, for the legs of her were
deep in the hole. He gave her no time to get out again
but quickly lunged forward with his sword and drove
it into her waistband, up to the very hilt. That was
the end of her!

It's like to be the end of Mac-an-Coill'uaine, too, he
said to himself as he let himself slip to the ground, for
was he dead? or was he alive? Had anyone asked him
he'd not be able to say. Then he heard the sound of
weeping, and the calling of his name, and it was pleasant to his ears, for what he heard were the voices of
his three foster brothers, seeking him among the dead.
He raised his own voice and called to them weakly,
and they came hurrying to his side.

"Are you not dead then, Mac-an-Coill'uaine?" they
asked.

"Not yet, but I will be," he answered, "unless you
go quickly and fetch the box of magic ointment that
lies on the ground beside the dead gruagach over there."

They fetched the box and he put some of the ointment on his finger and stuck it into his mouth, and a
moment after he was on his feet again, as strong and

153 ·

well as ever he had been. He dropped the box into his pouch, for a handy thing it would be, and then he picked up the sword of MacDeorcha and went over to him where he lay dead.

"This is the rogue who dared to put shame and dishonor upon the king," said he. With MacDeorcha's own sword, Mac-an-Coill'uaine cut off the head and the right hand of the dead man, and cut out his heart, stringing them all on a twig from a hazel tree, the better to carry them. He looked into MacDeorcha's pouch and there were the king's three teeth, which he put away safe in his own sporran.

The night was growing dark about them, for when MacDeorcha died the fire that ringed the island went out like a candle snuffed. It had been kindled by Mac-Deorcha with one of his magic spells, but when he was slain every spell he had laid was gone and all his wicked magic had no more power.

"The hours of the day just have worn me down to a shadow of myself," said Mac-an-Coill'uaine to his brothers. "It's myself is ready to rest." So back to the castle they made their way through the dark of the night, and laid themselves down to sleep.

When they arose in the morning, Mac-an-Coill'uaine said to his foster brothers, "Now you are free forever from all MacDeorcha's crosses and spells. Will you stay here or will you come back with me?"

"We will stay here," the brothers said. "There is no enchantment upon us now, and the island is ours for the taking, since MacDeorcha and all his sons are slain.

All MacDeorcha's lands and wealth and castles will belong to us. We shall found our own kingdoms on this island and be happy here. And you, too, if you will remain with us, shall have your own portion of all, share and share alike."

"I cannot stay," said Mac-an-Coill'uaine. "Though I should be well pleased to remain with you here and am not ungrateful for your generosity, I am bound by my oath to return to my king, for I have sworn cain to bring him the proof that the insult done him has been avenged. But how I can get away from here is another thing again, for it is too far to swim and I have no wings to fly, and the king's sons, may a black hour fall upon them!, took the ship we came in and sailed away."

"Do not trouble yourself about that," his foster brothers told him. "There is a corrach of MacDeorcha's on the shore which will carry you home again. 'Tis a very good little boat for it will sail of itself, and when you get back to your own land, if you turn its prow back toward this island, it will come sailing home to us."

Mac-an-Coill'uaine went down to the shore with the brothers, and there was the corrach, pulled up on the sands. He bade his foster brothers farewell, and setting the corrach on the water, with its prow turned homeward, he stepped into it and started on his journey, carrying with him the head and the hand and the heart of MacDeorcha, and the three teeth of the king.

If it took three days for the ship of the king's sons to reach the island, the corrach made the journey back

in less than one, so that Mac-an-Coill'uaine stepped
his foot on the sands of the shore of his own land before
the sun had set that day. He turned the prow of the
boat back toward the island and off it went at once,
and soon was out of sight. As he went up from the
shore he head a great screeching and howling from
the castle and he hurried his steps, for it was the voice
of the king he heard, and what was happening to him
he couldn't think.

Into the hall he went and there was the king at the
head of his table with the little jewel of a woman sitting beside him, at his right hand. And on the other
side of the king were his two sons, and they were trying
to fit into the king's jaws the three teeth of the old
horse, which they had stolen from Mac-an-Coill'uaine.
But the teeth, being the wrong ones, could not be made
to fit, and the king was screaming with the pain they
were giving him.

When the little jewel of a woman saw Mac-an-
Coill'uaine, she burst out laughing, and the king stopped
howling and turned to her in surprise.

"For seven days you've sat beside me at my table,"
said the king. "You've shared my food and my drink,
and in all that time you have never opened your lips
to say a word, nor laughed, nor even so much as cracked
a smile! Why do you laugh now?"

"Who would not laugh?" said the little jewel of a
woman, and she pointed her finger at Mac-an-Coill'-
uaine. "There is the hero!" she said. "Not your two sons,
who brought you the head and hand and heart of the

wrong man and the teeth of an old nag, all of which they stole from Mac-an-Coill-uaine himself. If I kept my tongue quiet before this, it was because I dared not speak, because your two sons said they would have my life if I said so much as a word. The real hero is here before you, and how he got here I cannot say, for they left him stranded on the island of fire when they sailed away."

Mac-an-Coill'uaine walked up to the king and laid before him the hazel twig on which the head and the heart and the hand of MacDeorcha, Son of Darkness, were strung. The king looked into the dead man's face and saw that it was indeed that of the man who had come riding behind the dark storm cloud.

Then Mac-an-Coill'uaine took from his pouch the three teeth of the king and the box with the magic ointment in it. He put a bit of ointment on each tooth, and slipped them, one by one, into the mouth of the king. Each tooth snapped back into its socket as if it had never been out, and the king felt no pain at all, they being the right teeth this time.

The king's sons turned red, then white, then green, for they had told their father a raft of lies about Mac-an-Coill'uaine, saying that he was a coward who stole the armor of the king's oldest son and took to his heels and ran away, leaving them to fight alone. They stood there, too terrified to move a foot, or say a word in their own defense—not that there was a word that they could have said. Then Mac-an-Coill'uaine took hold of them and bound them with the three points, of ankles, wrists, and waists, and threw them under the table among the dogs and candle drippings and the bits of waste food from the dishes on the table top above.

When the king understood what had happened, he was wild with rage. "By all the laws of truth and justice," said he, "these are no longer sons of mine!" He gave orders that they should be carried off to the dungeons, from which they should be taken to be hanged before the setting of the next day's sun.

If the king woke early the next morn, Mac-an-Coill'uaine woke earlier. Dawn had hardly cried itself in when the king opened his eyes, and there was Mac-an-Coill'uaine on his knees at the bedside, begging a boon from the king.

"There is naught in the world I would refuse you, Mac-an-Coill'uaine," the king said. "Name it and you shall have it, my man."

"It's not my way to be asking favors," said Mac-an-Coill'uaine. "Maybe I'd better not."

"Och, speak up!" said the king. "Whatever it is you want you shall have it. I promise you that."

Now that Mac-an-Coill'uaine had what he wanted, which was the promise of the king, he did not delay to ask for the boon he sought.

"Spare the lives of your sons, Your Majesty," said he.

"You are the last man in the world who should be asking me that," said the king. "But I have given my word. Their lives shall be spared. Still they must not go unpunished for the evil they have done. They're a wicked pair and unworthy to be my sons."

"Och," said Mac-an-Coill'uaine. "They are not so much wicked as foolish. And if all the men in the world who are fools should be hanged for their foolishness, I'm thinking there would not be many men left alive. Your Majesty, considering that, will not be too hard upon this pair."

"Och, well," said the king. "It shall be as you say. Fools they have been, and fools they shall ever be."

So the two king's sons were not hanged, but they were put into fools' dresses and each given a bauble to carry, and their hair was shaven from one side of their heads. Then they were turned out of the castle and all the dogs and the vagabonds in the place harried them out of the town, but not before Mac-an-Coill'uaine had made sure that each of them took with him a good big pouch of gold pieces so that they would not come to want. Folk say that they went into another kingdom where they became jesters at the court and being well thought of by the king there, were happy and quite contented to be fools.

As for Mac-an-Coill'uaine, he became chief steward of the king he had served so well. When he wedded the little jewel of a woman, the celebration was so grand that folk haven't stopped talking about it yet. The wedding lasted for seven days, and seven weeks, and seven months, and seven years, with folk coming and going all the time, and such feasting and merrymaking as had never been known before. But finally it ended and Mac-an-Coill'uaine and his little jewel of a woman settled down happily all the rest of their days.

The Sea Captain

ONCE a sea captain of the Western Isles by habits
of hard work and thrift was able to get enough money
together to buy a ship for himself. In this effort he was
helped by a legacy from an old aunt who loved him
well, and this gift with his savings made a long cher-
ished dream come true.

The ship was not one of these monstrous big ones,
but she was not so small that she could not hold a good-
sized cargo. As she was a trim and seaworthy craft,
she suited the captain fine, and he was well pleased to
be master of a ship of his own.

He sailed to foreign places, trading along the way,

and when he had a good load stowed away in the hold of his bonnie ship, he started back toward home. When he got back to the Isles he took a notion to carry his cargo to one of the big ports on the mainland, thinking he'd get a better price for his wares there than in one of the smaller ports of the Islands. He brought his ship in and anchored her by the quay, and then he went up to the harbor-master's office to let them know there that he'd put into the port and to pay his wharfage fees. While he was in the town he spread the word that he had a load of merchandise on board and would be willing to consider offers for it if anyone was minded to buy. Then he went back to his ship and set the crew to cleaning her up and touching up her paint. He liked a neat-looking ship, the captain did.

There was not much going on at the harbor that day, except for the activities of some fishermen who had just come in with their catch. The sea captain stood at the rail of his ship watching them unloading their fish and spreading their nets to dry, while he smoked a pipe, leaning lazily over the rail and enjoying the feeling of being owner of the ship whose deck was under his feet.

Having his eyes on the cobbled shore beyond the water's edge, he saw no one coming down to the quay, so it gave him such a surprise he nearly dropped his pipe into the sea when a voice hailed him from the wharf just below. But if he was surprised at hearing the voice that called up to him, that was nothing to the shock he got when he looked down and saw the man who stood below him on the quay.

The sea captain was not a small man, by any manner of means, but the stranger would have made two of him on any day of the week. He was easily twice the size of the captain, in height and heft and brawn. How he got there without the captain seeing him was something the captain couldn't understand. It was beyond reason to believe that his eye would not have caught sight of anyone as big as that coming down from the shore. The sea captain had seen some sizable men in his time, but he'd never laid eyes on one who was the match of this man.

The big fellow lifted a hand in a friendly sort of way, and the sea captain nodded politely to him. The two of them exchanged the usual courtesies, and for a while they discussed the weather and other commonplace matters, and then they got down to business.

"They're saying you've got a cargo you'd like to have taken off your hands," the big man said.

"Are they, now?" the sea captain answered. "Och, well! I'm in no great hurry to part with it, at all. There's naught that I have that will spoil on me if I hold it a while longer. Not that I would not consider an offer, if the price should suit me."

"Well, then, what is your cargo, and how much of it do you have?" the big man asked.

"There's salt," said the sea captain. "Four good hogsheads of that, and twice that of sugar, and a chest of

China tea. There's two score and ten bolls of fine wheaten flour, and of spices, ten canisters. Then, to please the ladies' taste, I've three bolts of sprigged muslin and one of the finest silk. It's a very fine lot of wares, to be sure, and all of it the finest quality to be found. And all of it sealed tight and made secure against the sea damp. But take it or leave it, as you please—it's all the same to me."

"I'll take the lot, if we can agree on a price," the big man said.

So they haggled over the price for a while, but at last they hit upon one that suited them both. The bargain was struck and then the big fellow said he'd want the goods set ashore, but not here at the quay, as he did not dwell in these parts. Would the captain be willing to carry them to the island where his home was? The captain was feeling so good about selling his whole cargo out-of-hand, and not some of it here and some of it there, as he had expected to do, that he agreed to do as the big man asked. So it was arranged that the sea captain would deliver the cargo, and the big man would pay for the wares as soon as they were unloaded at the big man's home port.

Well, then, the sea captain said, he'd be sailing his ship out on the next full tide so as to get the cargo where it was wanted as quick as he could. Let the big man just tell him where to go.

"Och, nay!" the big man said. "You'd ne'er find it from me telling you the way. The place is a far way off and hard to find. You'd only lose yourself."

"You'll have to be finding me a map, then," the sea captain said. "I've sailed to many a foreign port with naught but maps to guide me, and never lost myself as yet."

"Och, man, you'd not be finding the place on any map I know of," said the big man. "Look ye now—why should I not come along with you and show you the way myself?"

The sea captain had no objection to the big man's company, so the big man came on board the ship, and when the tide was full again, the sea captain hauled up his anchor and sailed his ship away.

When the ship came out from among the islands and faced the open sea the sea captain turned to the big man and asked him the way to go.

"Straight ahead," the big man said, "toward the westering sun."

So for three days and three nights the ship sailed westward, and then they came up to a great white bank of fog. The sea captain, eyeing the fog with little favor, asked the big man again which way to go.

"Straight ahead," the big man said.

The sea captain did not think highly of going into the fog, but he sailed his ship straight ahead, as the big man directed, and found to his surprise that although the fog was thick all around and about them there was wind to fill the sails and carry the ship forward. So for three days and three nights the ship sailed westward through the fog bank, and then they came to the end of it, and there was the open sea before them again, and far off across the sea to the west they saw the dim shape of land.

"There's the place we're going to," the big man said.

The sea captain headed his ship toward the land, and reached it just as night was falling on the seventh day of his voyage. He brought his ship in and anchored it beside a great stone pier that jutted out from the shore.

"You'll not be wanting to unload at this late hours," said the big man. " 'Twill soon be too dark to see what you are doing. Best leave it until the morn. Your crew will work with more of a will when they've put a good night's rest behind them."

Well, the sea captain admitted that what the big man said made sense. It wasn't as if he was in any great hurry to be on his way again, since he had sold his whole cargo to the big man and could afford to take his time about leaving. A few hours, more or less, would not matter at all.

So he and the big man had a nightcap together, and then the big man went up the shore and disappeared into the darkness of the night, and the sea captain went down to his cabin and went to bed.

When the sea captain woke in the morning he rose and went up to the deck to have a look at the place to which he had come. The sun was already up and the waves of the sea were tipped with its brightness, and the sky above was clear and blue. It looked like a grand fair day as far as the weather went. He turned his eyes from the sea to have a look at the land. At the first sight of it he nearly lost his breath at the loveliness that lay before him. In all his life he had never before beheld an island of such surpassing beauty.

Up above the shore stood what looked to be a village of big white houses, and there was a huge castle rising alone beyond the town. There were flourishing gardens about the houses and fine orchards where the fruit which grew on the trees was of an amazing size, and there were green fields of growing corn here and there. Behind the houses there was a wide stretch of moor glowing under the rays of the sun like a rippling purple river, and over it bees were busy at gathering honey from the bloom on the heather and humming contentedly the while. The moor ran well inland and beyond it lay a great forest of tall straight trees whose trunks seemed never to have been stunted or twisted by harsh winds from the sea. Among their green branches birds sang their early songs which in the morning stillness came faintly but sweetly to the captain's ears. The breezes which blew over the island were warm and gentle, and as laden with fragrance as if they had blown over vast extents of flowers in full bloom. Over all the island there was an air of calmness and peace. In all his travels the sea captain had never seen an island that could compare to this.

He stayed for a long time, lost in admiration, and might have stayed longer had he not suddenly remembered the cargo that was still to be unloaded. The big man was not in sight but the sea captain thought it would be well to get on with the job anyway.

He called his crew together and went with them to the hold, but when they opened the hatches he got a terrible shock! *The cargo was gone!* The hold was as empty as if it had been swept by a broom. There was not so much as a grain of salt or a drift of flour left in the place. There was no way of telling how he had done it, but nobody could doubt that the big man had made off with the whole of the sea captain's cargo during the dark hours of the night, while the crew and their captain slept.

The sea captain was not one to allow himself to be cheated out of what was rightfully his own. He bade the crew remain on the ship while he went up to the town to see if he could lay the thief by the heels, and get either his money or his wares back again.

At the top of the shore he found a lot of big houses with tall white walls and high thatched roofs. He went from house to house seeking the big man, but though he searched through every house there was nobody at all at home in a single one of them. There were fires burning on the hearths and kettles singing over the fires. There were pitchers of milk and fresh baked bannocks on the tables. Judging by the great size of everything he laid eyes upon—kettles, pitchers, bowls, tables, and chairs—the sea captain thought that all the people who dwelt in these house must be as oversized as the big man himself. But as for a living soul in any one of them at the time, there was not one to be found, upstairs or down. The sea captain came out of the last house with the wrath rising high in him. He stopped and looked about him and saw the huge castle that stood beyond the town.

"If he is not here, he might be there," he said, and off he started for the castle to look for the big man there.

When he came to the castle he went boldly in at the gate, and through the doorway of the castle into the hall. There he saw a man sitting at a table in the middle of the room, engaged in playing a game of chess against himself. The man wore a gold crown on his head and a velvet cloak hung from his shoulders. His garments were studded with precious stones from neck to hem and a sword in a golden sheath hung from his belt. If he was not bigger, he certainly was no smaller than the big man the sea captain sought. This will be the king of this land, without a doubt, the sea captain told himself.

The sea captain walked up to the table and said to the king, "Good day, and a blessing on the house and all within it."

Without looking up from his game the king answered, "Fáilte. Good day, and to you the same." And he took time to consider his next play and then moved one of the chessmen on his board. Then he raised his eyes and looked the sea captain full in the face. If the king was surprised to see a stranger before him and unannounced, he did not show it. He looked the sea captain over, leaning easily back in his chair the while. Then he said, "Fáilte! Welcome, stranger, if you come in peace. How did you find your way to this island?"

"I'm a sea captain by trade and I come from the

Western Isles," the captain said. "I was brought here
by a man of this place."

"You have come a far distance," said the king. "But
why have you come here to me?"

"I seek justice," the sea captain answered. "I have
been tricked and cheated by the man who brought
me to your island, and though I have searched through
the village for him he was not to be found."

"You shall have justice if you deserve it," said the
king. "But first we must take some food together, and
when we have eaten, I will listen to what you have to
say."

Then the king pushed his chessboard aside, and called
some big serving lasses, bidding them bring food, which
they did. They set huge platters of bread and meat
upon the table, and bowls of golden and red apples
so large that the sea captain could scarcely hold one
of them in his two cupped hands. Tall flagons of wine
were set beside them, but when the sea captain came
to take his up he found that he could not lift it from
its place on the table, so heavy it was. The king, seeing
the trouble he was having, called one of the big lasses
and she held the flagon up to the sea-captain's lips so
that he might drink his wine. For all that, the sea
captain made a very good meal, and when they had
finished eating and the food was cleared from the
table, the king leaned forward and setting his elbows
on the table said, "Now I will listen to what you have
to say and we'll soon have your troubles sorted out."

So the sea captain told the king everything that had

happened from his first meeting with the big man on the quay on the mainland to this same morning when he opened the hatches of the hold and discovered that his cargo was gone. The king's brow grew black as thunder as he listened, and when the sea captain had finished he flew into such a rage as made the sea captain bless his fate that it was another man who had roused the king to anger, and not himself.

"Would you be knowing this fellow if you saw him again?" asked the king, when his wrath had cooled off a bit.

"Know him?" the sea captain said. "Och, I'd know him if twenty years had passed since last I saw him, and not just one night."

Then the king sent forth word to say that all the men on the island, barring none, whatever their occupation, must come at once to the castle, and when they had come he bade them form themselves into a line and pass, one by one, by the table where he and the sea captain sat. They were a fine-looking lot, the men of the island, every one of them as big as the big man who had brought the sea captain there, and some were even bigger. Tall, they were, and strong, and ruddy with health. Although they walked by slowly, as the king told them to do, there was no shuffling along, but each man moved with a light confident step, and every face was cheerful and serene. The sea captain looked them over from the beginning of the line to the end, but he did not see the big man he was seeking for anywhere at all.

And if he did not see the big man, there was a very good reason, for in his travels away from the island the big man had picked up a bit of magic, and now the rascal had laid upon himself a spell which made him invisible to the sea-captain's eyes. The big man dared not use his spell all the time, lest the king notice his absence and ask why he was not in the line with the other men. When the king looked his way, he let himself be seen, but when the sea captain turned his head toward him he took refuge and hid himself in his spell. He was having a lively time of it, changing back and forth, and counting himself lucky that the king and the captain did not look toward him at the same time, but the sea-captain's luck turned out to be better than his own. Just as the captain was about to give up and say good-by to his cargo, he caught, from the corner of his eye, a glimpse of something moving just beyond the last man in the line. It was a misty, wavering shape, but the sea captain knew who it was, without taking time to think about it.

"There's the fellow that cheated me out of my cargo," he said to the king. "Down there at the end of the line!"

The king looked, and there was the big man coming along after the rest of them, trying to look as unconcerned as the rest. But the king called him by name, and order him to step up to the table, and the others he sent away. Then the king said to the big man, "This sea captain from the outside world claims that you brought him here by trickery and stole his cargo away. What have you got to say for yourself?"

The big man said nothing, and what could he say? His guilt showed in his face.

Then the king gave the big man a look that was heavy with anger and contempt. "Woe to the day," said the king, "upon which I brought you to this place. You have ever been a maker of mischief and given too much to going about the world that lies away from our island. You have no place in our land of peace. Never shall it be said that one of us has stooped to thieving and trickery. You shall pay dearly for your misdeeds."

Then the king turned to the sea captain. "What price was agreed upon for the cargo?" he asked, and the sea captain told him. Then the king said to the big man, "This price you shall pay, but you shall pay more, for you shall pay the price three times over. Lay the money before me at once that I may make sure that there is no mistake in your count."

So the big man had to take out of his pouch three times the price he had agreed to pay for the cargo, and put it on the table before the king, and a very big pile it made, too. The king counted the golden coins and when he had made sure that the sum was what it ought to be, he pushed them over to the sea captain. "Take it up," said the king, "and put it in your pocket."

"Och, nay!" the sea captain protested. "Fair's fair! I want no more than what's rightly mine. The price alone suits me well enough."

"Take it up!" commanded the king. " 'Tis your own

and my blessing is on it. One part is for the cargo, but the other two parts are the penalty for theft according to the ancient law of the people of the Finne. It is the *Cothram na Fiantachd*, the Fair Play of the Finne."

Well, if the king said he must take the money, then he must, the sea captain thought. So he picked up the coins and put them away in his pouch.

"As for you," the king said to the big man, "your greed has brought shame upon us and blackened the fame of us all. You are not fit to abide here with honest men. This day ends your life on this island, and where you go when you depart from us we do not ask nor care to know. Only make sure that you never try to return. A boat, from among those at the shore, you may have to leave in, and beside that only what you can carry in a sack on your back. Go now—and go quickly!"

The big man slunk off, shamefaced, to pack his sack, and the king turned back to the sea captain and talked with him pleasantly for a while, until a man came up from the shore to say that the tide was right and the wind was fair, if the sea captain would like to take advantage of them and start on his voyage home.

The king walked down to the pier with the sea captain to bid him Godspeed on his way. As they were going down the shore to the ship, along behind them came the big man with his sack of belongings on his back. He came up close beside the sea captain and said softly in his ear, "Tell me, man, which eye did you see me with when I was at the end of the line in there?"

It was right on the tip of the sea captain's tongue to say, "It was with both of my eyes I saw you." He never knew what it was that kept him from it, but something kept the words back in his mouth. "It was my left eye that caught sight of you," the sea captain said, which was the truth, to be sure, but the right eye had seen as much as the left.

The big man quickly raised a hand and poked a finger into the sea captain's left eye. It did not hurt at all, but it took the sight entirely from the captain's left eye, and that eye was forever blind. There was no way of mending it, once it was done, but the sea captain counted himself as being lucky because he had been wise enough not to say he had seen the big man with both his eyes. There is no doubt that the big man would have made sure, if he had, that the captain would have lost the sight of both his eyes instead of only one.

When they came down to the pier the king stopped them, and bade them brush their shoes, both uppers and soles. The sea captain couldn't make out why the king was so careful about it, but if it was what the king wanted him to do, he didn't mind. So they brushed their shoes, himself and the big man, until they were clean as a whistle, with no more dust upon them than if they'd just come from the cobbler's hands. Then the sea captain boarded his ship and the big man stepped into a corrach that was tied up by the pier. The sea captain sailed off one way and the big man sailed off the other, and that was the last the sea captain ever saw of him.

The sea captain waved good-by to the king on the shore, and then he turned his ship to the east and sailed away from the island. The ship sailed back the way it had come, over the open sea, and through the fog bank, and out to the open sea again, going eastward all the time. On the seventh day, at nightfall, the sea captain came safely home to the Western Islands and anchored his ship at his own home port. And if he did not have the big man to guide him, it did not matter at all, for though without guide and without chart, he had no trouble in finding his way.

The sea captain left his ship and went up to the tavern above the shore, and there he found a number of seafarers gathered, comparing notes on the travels from which they had just returned. The sea captain sat down among them and added the tale of his voyage to those that the other sailors told. The other sea captains listened in wondering silence to what the sea captain said about his adventures with the big man, and they marveled at what he told them about the beauty of that island in the far western sea.

Then one very old seaman who had sailed the seas for many long years spoke up, saying, "I know of that island. Myself, I have never laid my eyes upon it, but I have met many who have spoken of sailing westward and seeing in the far distance the misty shapes of its trees and houses and towers. Until this day I have heard of no man who succeeded in reaching its shores. That island is Eilean-h-oige, the Isle of Youth, where all is fair, where no one ever dies, and it is peopled by saints and heroes and great men. That just king you met was Fionn himself, who dwells there with his companions. He made you clean your shoes before you left so that no grain of dust from the island might remain upon them lest it lead you back to the Isle of Youth again."

The old seaman must have been right in what he said. Over and over, through the years, the sea captain tried to find his way back, but he never laid eyes upon the island again. However, he still had the gold the king had made the big man hand over to him, and the blessing of Fionn upon it must have been a power for good. Every venture the sea captain used it for brought him good fortune so that he became a wealthy man.

The sea captain remembered, all the rest of his life, and with great longing, that island in the far western sea, with its moor glowing purple in the sunlight and the bees humming over the heather. He remembered its fair gardens and orchards and green fields of grain, and its tall forests where birds sang all the day. And always he remembered the air of peace and calmness that hung over all.

He never forgot the big man, either, although he never met with him again. If he had been inclined to forget him—which he was not—he had a token to remind him. His left eye, into which the big man had poked his finger, was blind to the end of the days.

A Bauchan in the Family

FOLK who travel by the boat that runs to the Isle of Skye, when they have come up the Sound of Mull past Tobermory, will round the Point of Ardnamurchan. As they come around the point they will see three islands before them which have names that sound very odd to strangers' ears. These are the isles of Rum and Eigg and Muck.

The Isle of Rum is wild, rugged, and rocky, with little on it but a few scattered crofts and fishermen's cottages, and the ruins of an ancient monastery said to have been built by the holy Columba himself. On Eigg there's a grand mountain of a very queer shape that's called the Scaur Eigg, and a causeway, the pillars of which are near to nine hundred feet high, and a wonderful sight it is to see. On Eigg is the Cave of the Massacre, where two hundred men, women, and children of the MacDonald clan were slain in a clan feud hundreds of years ago. The cave in which they died became their tomb forever after and their bones still lie there. These two of the three, therefore, have some small claim to fame.

The third island, the Isle of Muck, has little of note about it, being remarkable only for being the place where all the population got together and left one day, never to come back any more. For long years the island has lain deserted, a region of lonely moorland covered with twisted heather, gorse, and blackthorn, with here and there the remnants of bits of run-down pasture land where the grass grows coarse. The cliffs along the shore are stern and unfriendly, and by day and by night the sea wind blows unkindly over the isle with a lash of snow on the end of its tail in winter, and a lash of rain all the rest of the year.

It was never a comfortable place to bide in, nor a place where a living was easy to win, but there once was a time when there were plenty of people living on the Isle of Muck. There were between thirty and forty families, about one hundred and fifty souls in all. With one exception, these folk were divided about evenly between two clans, the MacDonalds and the MacLeods, whose members had dwelt on the island for so many generations that the date of the arrival of their ancestors was long lost in the mists of the ancient days. Whether the MacDonalds or the MacLeods had been the first to land there was a bone of contention over which the two clans fought all the way to the day that they finally left Muck for good.

It was hardly worth wasting the breath it took to carry the argument on, because by intermarriage the two families had become so mixed up with each other that it would have been difficult to sort them out. All of them, MacLeods and MacDonalds alike, were either grandfathers, grandmothers, fathers, mothers, aunts, uncles, sisters, brothers, or cousins anywhere from first- to twenty-times removed of one another, so the kinship among the folk of the two clans was terribly confused. The truth was that every MacLeod on Muck had a wide streak of MacDonald to him, and every MacDonald on Muck had a wide streak of MacLeod to him, but de'il a one of them would have admitted the same.

The one exception was a family that belonged to the MacIntosh clan. How they ever got on the Isle of Muck with all the MacLeods and the MacDonalds is a mystery that has not been solved to this day. However it happened, this family had dwelt on Muck as long as the MacLeods and the MacDonalds, and maybe longer, for all that anyone knows. They were a proud stubborn lot, very much given to keeping themselves to themselves, so they never had anything much to do with the MacDonalds or the MacLeods, beyond passing a civil "good day" should they happen to meet.

Through the generations, the MacIntosh family

dwindled. They grew fewer and fewer as the years went by until at last there was only one representative of the family left, and that one was the Young MacIntosh of this tale.

When his mother and father died off on him, both about the same time, they left him all they had of the MacIntosh possessions, and if it was not a great fortune, it could well have been less. They left him a bit of a cottage with some furnishings to it, and a byre and a shed. They left him a money kist, and it not too badly filled, because his folk had always had saving habits, and there were a couple of cows and a small flock of sheep. These things, with a few family heirlooms in the shape of jewelry and clothing that had been handed down from one generation to another, made up the inheritance of Young MacIntosh. On the whole it was not bad for a lad just starting out to make his own way through life. But in addition to these, there was something else he inherited from his mother and father, and that was the bauchan that belonged to the MacIntosh family.

Maybe you have ne'er seen a bauchan, and maybe you have without knowing what it was you saw. Happen you'd be going across the moor or along the shore by the sea and, looking before you, yo'd spy a wee person some way ahead. The creature would be no more than three feet high, standing on its toe points, and a body'd be thinking it was a bairn until the wee fellow turned his head to look back at you over his shoulder. You'd know that minute that this was no bairn. You could tell by the wrinkles and furrows in the old face, and the hair and the beard that were grizzled with age. He'd give you a glare with eyes that were so bright and hot that a body'd think they'd burn a hole right through one, and then with a scowl and a growl he'd slip away, behind a thorn bush or an outcrop of rock, and be seen no more.

Then you'd stop in your tracks and say, "Och, Heaven preserve us! 'Twas a bauchan that I saw there. That one was no mortal at all." And you would be right. A bauchan it was. They are queer ones, the bauchan people, because although they are *cinneadh do'n sighideach,* that is true kin to the fairies, they will not live with their own folk, but choose to make their homes among men. Nevertheless, they are fairy persons, and always will be till time ends.

This bauchan that Young MacIntosh inherited from his parents had belonged to the MacIntosh family for hundreds and hundreds of years. Nobody ever knew what his age was, but as he never seemed to get any older as the generations of MacIntoshes were born and lived and died, always remaining at the same stage of old age through the centuries as far as anybody could see, the family asked no questions, but took him as he was. He was a *grummilie,* dour old creature, but he was greatly attached to the branch of the MacIntosh family that lived on Muck, having come there with the ancestor who first settled on that isle. When he was in a good mood he was always ready to give them a helping hand.

All the MacIntoshes in the past generations had been

quiet peaceable folk who suited the bauchan well. The father of Young MacIntosh had been a well-mannered, soft-spoken man, not at all the sort to set up difficulties, so he and the bauchan got along fine. It wasn't until he was dead and Young MacIntosh took over the croft that the bauchan began to fear that things were not going to be the way they had been in the father's day.

Young MacIntosh was one of those redheaded, quick-tempered lads, easily offended and always ready with his fists. He was stocky in build but strong, and well able to hold his own in any sort of fight. He and the bauchan were very well matched. What the bauchan lacked in height he more than made up for by his terrible strength and the quickness with which he was able to get around. MacIntosh was his better in having a well-earned skill at placing his blows, and longer arms. As soon as Young MacIntosh came into the property he and the bauchan sized each other up and anybody could see with half an eye that either one of them was ready to fight as soon as the other one gave the word.

As might be expected, after that, some of the time the bauchan and the new master of the croft would work along together side by side, and if they were not what you could call friendly, at least they were at peace. Then something would set them at odds, and all of a sudden the two of them would be slogging away at each other with fists and feet. Neither was able ever to get the best of the other, so nobody ever won the fight. They just kept at it until both of them were too worn out to go on any longer and then they stopped.

After a few weeks of living in the cottage with only the bauchan for company, Young MacIntosh took it into his head to find a wife for himself. In the past when one of the MacIntoshes wanted to wed he went over to the mainland to pick out a likely young cousin from among the MacIntoshes there for a wife, and brought her home to the Isle of Muck. For some reason or other Young MacIntosh decided not to follow the family custom, but to look closer to home for a bride. Maybe he had not the inclination to make the long journey to the mainland to look up his kinsmen, but it is more likely that his decision was made for a different reason. Anybody on Muck might have noticed, if they had been in at noticing mood, that for a long time he'd been keeping his eye on a bonnie lassie named Morag MacLeod, who lived in the village nearby.

The bauchan was terribly vexed when Young Mac-Intosh told him what he had in his mind. "Och, have ye no pride, man?" demanded the bauchan. "Never in the history of the family was there a time when a MacIntosh took up with a MacLeod. Are there no MacIntosh lassies left on the mainland for you to wed?"

"Happen there are," Young MacIntosh said. "I'm not fashing myself to find out. There wouldn't be one that would suit me as well as bonnie wee Morag MacLeod."

"I have lived hundreds of years," the bauchan told him, "and all my life long I've watched the MacLeods and the MacDonalds going their own gait on this island, and the MacIntoshes doing the same, always keeping themselves to themselves. Will you bring shame

on the good folks who went before you by bringing in
a MacLeod?"

Young MacIntosh only laughed. "There will be no
MacLeod in the family," he said. "And I'll tell you why.
From the minute we're wedded Morag MacLeod will
be a MacLeod no longer. She will be Morag MacIntosh."

It didn't sound quite right to the bauchan, and yet,
in a sense, it was true. He wrinkled his brow and his
nose with a terrible frown and muttered to himself
while Young MacIntosh got himself ready to go courting
Morag MacLeod.

"Och, well," said the bauchan at last. "Happen she'll
not have you. Even a MacLeod or a MacDonald would
have to be out of her wits entirely before she'd take up
with a worthless coof like yourself."

The lad only laughed. "I'll thrash you tomorrow for
what you have said today," he said. And off he went
to the village to seek for the lass he was hoping to wed.

If Young MacIntosh had his eye upon Morag Mac-
Leod, she had been keeping her own upon him. His red
hair and his bold ways had taken her fancy and it
was not in his disfavor that he had a good little croft
of his own. She had always admired a lad with plenty
of spirit and she could see that he had enough and to
spare. She made up her mind she'd have him for a
husband, providing he asked her, of course, so when he
asked her to be his wife she didn't stop to think it over,
but said at once that she would.

If the bauchan had been put out at the notion of a

MacIntosh wedding a MacLeod, it was nothing to the way Morag's kinsmen and connections took on about it. The MacLeods nearly went wild when Morag told them what she meant to do. But Morag, for all that she was a wee thing, had a mind of her own.

"I'm of an age to choose for myself the man I wish to marry," said she. "You cannot stop me, so you will have to make the best of it with a good grace."

She said it often enough for the MacLeods to see that she meant it, so they gave in and settled down again in the end. Then the MacLeods and the Mac-Donalds got together and gave Morag and Young MacIntosh a big wedding that lasted a week, with mountains of food and seas of drink to it. The MacLeods and the MacDonalds spent a good bit of time during the celebration engaging in fights with each other, when they weren't fighting among themselves, but all of them took great pains to be very civil to Young MacIntosh, and everybody had a grand time.

At the end of the week when the wedding was over and the new-wedded pair were on their way home, Young MacIntosh said to Morag, "I'm thinking there's something I haven't told you before."

"What would it be, lad?" Morag asked.

"Well, I've got an ugly wee bauchan at home, and I don't doubt he's going to be a trouble to you," MacIntosh said.

"Och, 'tis no news you're telling me," Morag said with a laugh. "Is there anybody on the Isle of Muck doesn't know about the bauchan that belongs to the MacIntosh family? Och, then, I was still in the cradle when I heard of him first."

"He's a mean wee de'il. I'd not like him to be vexing you," Young MacIntosh said.

"Do not fash yourself! Me and the bauchan will get on fine together. I'll soon get the wee fellow sorted out—just wait and see," said Morag. "If you had a dozen like him I'd not be bothered at all." And when you remember that wee Morag had got the best of all the MacLeods and MacDonalds when it came to a question of whom she was going to wed, maybe a grummilie bauchan didn't matter at all.

A house with no woman to tend it soon gets into a terrible state. When Morag saw what the housekeeping of a man and a bauchan had done to that one which Young MacIntosh brought her home to, she sighed and shook her head.

" 'Tis no fit place for human beings to dwell in," she declared. She started in with a will to put everything to rights, and for a while she was so busy she never gave the bauchan a thought. But after a week of scrubbing and sweeping and polishing had gone by, and everything was fresh and clean and bright, the way it ought to be, she remembered the little man.

"Where in the world would the bauchan be?" she asked. "Not so much as the shadow of the wee creature have I seen since I came."

"No more have I," Young MacIntosh said. "And I'll

tell you the truth—he may stay away forever, for all o' me. I'm weary of putting up with his sulks."

"Och, do not say so!" cried Morag. "Where would we be without the wee bauchan? Does he not belong to the family?"

Morag learned from Young MacIntosh that the bench by the hearth was considered by the bauchan to be his own property. She made a fine soft pillow and left it lying on the end of the bench that was nearest the fire. Every morn and every eve she set a big bowl of porridge and a dish of bannocks beside the pillow on the bench, but day by day she had to take the food away again, untouched. Morag was troubled because the bauchan stayed away, but still she waited, and hoped for his return. All her life she had heard folk talk of the MacIntosh's bauchan, and of his queer goings-on. Was she not to see him now, and she a MacIntosh herself? It vexed her sorely to think that maybe it was her coming that had driven him away.

Then one day she did see him, standing by the doorpost, peeping into the room. She made no sign that she knew he was there lest he flit away. He watched for a while as she went about her work, then growing bolder, he came a step or two farther into the house and looked around the room. Then his eye lit upon the pillow that lay on the bench.

He went over to the bench and picked up the pillow. "What would this be?" he growled, holding it out at arm's length.

"Och, 'tis naught but a wee pillow for your weary old bones," Morag said.

The bauchan sniffed and said scornfully, "It's hundreds of years that I've been in this family, and I do not remember anybody ever giving my bones a thought before!" But he laid the pillow back again in its place.

"Well, 'tis high time then that somebody did," said Morag.

Then the bauchan saw the big bowl of porridge and the bannocks that Morag had set out on the bench. "What's these for?" he asked.

"You did not come in for your dinner," Morag answered. "I put out the porridge and cakes in case you'd be wanting a piece, should you come in."

The bauchan said nothing, but he took up the bowl and ate the porridge and then he finished the bannocks to the last crumb. After he had eaten, he curled up on the pillow and lay on the bench by the fire, listening to Morag singing as she went about her work.

Things soon settled down into their ordinary ways, with Young MacIntosh and the bauchan working the croft together, and fighting together, by turns, and with Morag busy with her woman's work.

The bauchan seemed to have nothing more to say about the shame of bringing a MacLeod into the family. Although he scolded and scowled as much as ever, and muttered mightily to himself, many a time Morag's work was lighter because of his helping hand. When the weather was bad she never had to trudge over the moor seeking the cattle to bring them in to shelter. The two cows would be at the gate of the yard, waiting for her to lead them into the byre, and if it was not the bauchan who saw to it that they were brought up to the gate it was nobody else. And when Morag took her sack and spud and pail down to the shingle to pick whelks from the sands to sell on the mainland, who would be there but the bauchan with his own sack full to the top.

"Och, you're a late comer," he'd say. "Give me your sack, woman, and take my own instead. I do not want the whelks. They're no good at all, and fit only for folks on the mainland that know no better to eat. I ne'er could abide a whelk myself." And he'd skip about picking more whelks from the sand until he had filled her empty sack. Then he'd shoulder sacks, spuds, and pails and all, and urge her up the path before him, leaving her nothing to carry. " 'Tis no job for a lassie, gathering whelks," he'd scold. "MacIntosh should think shame to send you out for the whelks in the damp and the cold. Go back in the house, now, and tend to your knitting!"

Morag, who had picked whelks from the time that she was a wee bit of a lassie without any objection being offered, smiled to herself. But she said nothing, and went back to the house as she was told. She knew that the bauchan was showing in his dour way that he had decided that Morag was a MacIntosh and not a MacLeod.

There came a drear day of autumn when the bauchan and Young MacIntosh had a great fight about the proper way to tar a boat. Both of them tried to get hold of the brush and the tar in order to do the job right. But with two persons and two ways and only one brush and one bucket of tar, trouble could be expected, and soon it came. From a battle with words, it turned into a battle with fists, and there the two of them were, dinging and danging away at each other, and that the tar bucket got kicked over in the heat of the fight did not help in the least. The fight went on all morning and nobody won. They gave up at last with their strength near spent, and took the rest of the day to rest.

"Och, you've been at it again," sighed Morag when her man came in. "Look, now, lad, you'd better ease up on the fighting. There was none of it in your father's time. You'll drive the mannie away, so you will. One of these days he'll go off and leave you, if you drive him too far."

"Leave me!" exclaimed Young MacIntosh. " 'Twould be the best day of my life, should he go!"

"Now, lad, you'd be lost without him," Morag said. "Och, he's been forever in the MacIntosh family."

"Have I not enough to vex me without you nattering at me too?" Young MacIntosh asked. So Morag held her tongue, no matter what she thought to herself. She gave the two warriors mutton fat to take the tar off themselves, and comforted them with hot tea and oat cakes, and left them to rest.

That same day, when Morag came in just before nightfall from putting the cows in the byre, she asked, "Have you seen the storm clouds in the sky? I do not think I've ever before seen them so big and black. I'm thinking they'll let a load of snow down upon us soon. It grows colder, forbye."

"Whisht, woman!" Young MacIntosh said. "We'll have no snow. 'Tis far too early in the season for snow."

Morag cast an anxious eye at the heap of peats in the corner by the hearth. "There's not many peats left in the shed," she said. "If it turns bad and we have snow heavy on the ground, what we have will hardly see us through. Should we go down to the peat hag maybe, and bring us up a couple of loads?"

Young MacIntosh was still feeling sore from the drubbing he'd got from the bauchan that day. "Did I not tell you to hauld your whisht, woman?" he shouted. "I'm telling you we'll not have snow!"

Morag wanted no strife under the roof of her dwelling, so she said no more, but busied herself getting ready the evening meal.

When they had eaten the bauchan slipped out of the house, and when, after a while, he came in again, he said, "I've been gathering the sheep together and putting them in the byre. 'Tis well that somebody in this family has the wit to be weatherwise."

Young MacIntosh tossed up his head and glared at the bauchan and the bauchan glared back.

" 'Tis snowing," the bauchan said.

Young MacIntosh strode to the door and threw it

open. The snow was coming down, white and heavy, and already lay thick on the ground. He'd been wrong about the weather, even if he'd not admit it. The worst of it was that a snow like this might last for weeks—even all winter if the autumn frosts were bad, and the weather turned cold.

Morag came and laid her hand on his arm, drawing him into the house and shutting the door. "Do not fash yourself about it, lad," she said. "We'll make do with what we have. We'll get along."

So Young MacIntosh went back to the fire and sat down and thought what a coof he'd been not to take Morag's word for it and go fetch the peats before it began to snow. Neither he nor Morag noticed that the bauchan was gone again.

All of a sudden they heard a great bumping and thumping in the shed outside. They rushed to the window to look, and there was the bauchan dumping a huge load of peats from his back into the shed.

"I brought up all the peats we had cut," he shouted. "If there had been more I could have brought them too. But I doubt you'll be needing more anyway. The shed's full up." He came into the house stamping his feet and shaking the snow from his clothes. "I fancy a warm fire, myself," he said as he climbed up on his bench. Then curling up on his pillow, he went to sleep.

Young MacIntosh pulled on his boots and went out to the shed. When he came back he told Morag, " 'Tis true. The shed is so full you could not find room for so much as one more peat."

"Would you believe it!" said Morag. "He's brought the whole winter's store of peats on his wee back."

"I cannot say I'm not grateful to him. He's none so bad if you get on the right side of him," said Young MacIntosh. That was as close as he was willing to get to admitting that he had been wrong.

That was a bad autumn that year, with a wicked winter that came after and stayed long. The storms and the snows of it seemed to go on without end. When summer came at last, it was little better, for the weather was so wet and cold and windy the crops could not take hold. The haystacks had to be held down by ropes weighted with stones to keep the gales from blowing them into the sea, and the seed went into the ground and stayed there, and never came up at all. Men came back from the fishing with a catch hardly worth bringing in. The folk on Muck were fair disgusted, and with good reason, too.

Just when they were most disheartened, one of the MacDonalds, who had gone off to America ten years or so before, came back to the Isle of Muck to pay a visit to his family. You never saw a man so changed in your life. He was clad in a fine suit made by a city tailor, and his boots were fashioned of leather and polished until they shone. He had money clinking away in his pocket, and a silver watch at his side. The tales he told about the country across the water were almost beyond believing. There was a tract that they called the Western Reserve where there were forests of tall green trees and great tracts of waving grass as far as the eye could see. The soil, he said, was rich and deep with hardly a rock in a whole day's plowing, and all of it so cheap to buy it almost seemed like a gift.

First one islander and then another found his imagination catching fire. The de'il could have the Isle of Muck and they'd be going to the New World, to try their fortune there. The notion spread like wildfire and in no time at all every MacLeod and MacDonald on Muck had his mind made up to go to the country far over the sea.

When Young MacIntosh learned that they were planning to flit from Muck, he was neither to hold nor to bind. "Did you ever hear the like?" he demanded. "The lot of them to go off and leave us behind on this mischancy forsaken isle!"

"Muck was good enough for your forebears," said the bauchan. "Will you quarrel with their memories by calling it out of its name?"

"The de'il take Muck!" said Young MacIntosh. "What is it to me but a trouble and a torment—like yourself!"

"I'll remember you said that, MacIntosh," said the bauchan.

"Do so!" said MacIntosh. "If the MacLeods and the MacDonalds leave here, I'll not stay behind. I'm going along."

"So you'll shame the honest men who went before you, and them turning over in their graves to hear of a MacIntosh truckling to a MacDonald or a MacLeod!" the bauchan said.

"Who's truckling?" demanded Young MacIntosh. "I've as much right to go to America as any of them."

"It's not your going I mind," the bauchan said. "But must ye trail along after them like a laddie hanging on to his mither's shawl?"

"Och, havers!" said Young MacIntosh in disgust. "The ship will carry the lot of us at a very cheap rate compared with what it would cost if each man took passage for his family alone. I'll save good money by going along with them."

"What a man will do to put a few pennies in his pocket!" the bauchan said scornfully. "Och, well! I'll have naught to do with it. Go your own gait. I'll be leaving you in the morn."

True to his word, the next morning the bauchan bundled up his pillow and his bowl, with a sackful of fresh bannocks Morag had baked for him. He tied the bundle up and slung it over his shoulder, and went to the door.

"Good-by, all!" he said with a jaunty wave of his hand, and off he went.

Morag and Young MacIntosh watched him going along the path that led to the village. There were tears in Morag's eyes. "Och, he looks such a wee creature!" she said. "Go after him, lad, and fetch him home again."

"That I'll not," said MacIntosh. "Dinna fash yourself, lass. He'll not go far. You'll see the wee fellow creeping back to his warm corner when it comes time to go to bed."

"He'll not come back," Morag said slowly. "It's in my heart that we shall not see him again. You should not have told him he was a trouble to you, lad."

Night came, and morning followed, and more nights and mornings came after, one by one, but the bauchan did not return, either by day or by night. He was not mentioned at the croft but he was missed, all the same. The preparations that went on for the flitting were being carried along at a terrible rate and there was a great commotion in every house on the isle. The cattle and sheep were taken by boat to the mainland and sold to crofters there, along with anything else the islanders would not be wanting to carry along to America, for which they could find a sale. The houses were stripped and all that could be moved was packed or sold or given away. The last day came, and every one of the islanders, one hundred and fifty or more, men, women, and children, left the Island of Muck.

The last to board the ship as it lay in harbor at the mainland were Morag and Young MacIntosh. If the two of them hung back a little, maybe it was because, without mentioning it, each was hoping to the last that a wee body with a grummilie, scowling face would come along, and grumble at them for lagging behind. But the bauchan did not show himself, and they boarded the ship just in time to keep it from going off to America without them.

The long voyage, by sailing vessel in those days, was slow and dull. By good fortune, there were no storms, and at last the ship came safely into port. If Morag and Young MacIntosh were the last on board at the beginning of the journey, they were first off the ship at the end, so anxious they were to have the feel of solid ground under their feet.

They stood on the dock with their bundles piled about them, half-dazed with all the stir about them and half-frightened out of their lives by the strangeness of everything, looking around with wide eyes. Then, of a sudden, Morag clutched Young MacIntosh by the arm.

"Look, lad!" she cried. *"What do you see?"*

Young MacIntosh looked. What did he see but the bauchan, capering about on the wharf just beyond. "You can have your emigrant ship with your MacLeods and your MacDonalds! I got to America before you, MacIntosh," the bauchan shouted. "Maybe you saved a few pennies on your passage, lad, but I did better. Mine cost me nothing at all!"

Young MacIntosh said not one word in reply. Down on his knees he plumped and threw his arms open, and the bauchan rushed across the wharf and into Young MacIntosh's embrace.

All the folks on the dock turned to stare at Young MacIntosh and the queer-looking wee body hugging each other as if they'd never let go, while Morag stood behind them with her arms on their shoulders, and the tears running down her face.

"Praise be to God!" cried Morag. "The bauchan's come back to the MacIntosh family!"

The wee rascal had taken a ship that sailed a full week before their own, and as for the cost of his passage, the sly little bauchan had stowed away and not paid a penny for his fare.

All the MacLeods and the MacDonalds, and the MacIntosh family gathered up their gear and traveled west to take up homesteads in the New World there. The land was all they had been told, with tall green forests and wide sweeps of green waving grass. There was plenty of work to be done, hewing down trees, and clearing and breaking up the land, but losh! 'twas easy compared with what they'd had against them on the Isle of Muck. And Young MacIntosh was lucky. The bauchan gave him a helping hand.

All the MacLeods and the MacDonalds got along fine in the New World, but the MacIntosh family got along best of all. The bauchan and Young MacIntosh patched up their differences for good, both of them being too happy to fight. Young MacIntosh made his fortune and grew rich and respected, but he never took the credit to himself.

"If a man seeks to do well," he always said, "he'd best have a bauchan in his family."

GLOSSARY

Glossary

ain: own.
baile-beag: (bă'-ĭllah-bĕg'), a small farm village.
bairn: child.
bannocks: oatcakes.
bauchan: (baw'-hawn), one of the fairy people.
beannachadh: (bȳ-ann'-ăk-ah), a blessing.
beg: little.
bittock: a little bit.
blatherskate: a talker of nonsense.
blethering: silly talk.
boll: a sack usually containing flour to the weight of forty
    pounds.
bothan: (baw'-hawn), a hut.
boxbed: a bed built into the wall of a room, sometimes closed
    off by curtains, but sometimes by wooden doors.
bracken: a large fern.
brogues: boots.
burn: stream, brook.
but and a ben: a front room and a back room.
byre: a barn. A shelter for farm animals.
caddies: porters, errand boys.
cailleach: (kăly'-ak), an old woman.
cain: (cah-enn), a duty, a responsibility. To "lay cain upon
    oneself" means to give solemn promise.
cas-fionna: (cass'-fenna), curly-furred.

ceabharnach: (keh-vur'-nawk), a naughty breeze.

ceilidh: (kay'-lee), a gathering; a party; a merrymaking; a visit.

ceud: (keh-ad), a hundred.

ceud mile fáilte: (keh-ad mee-al fahl-tcha), a hundred thousand welcomes. (This is a friendly greeting.)

claidheamh: (clў̆-īve), sword.

Claidheamh-geal-solus: (clў̆'-īve-gyal-sölús), White Sword of Light.

coof: a fool.

corrach: (caw'-răk), a small, very light boat made of hides stretched on a wicker frame, round in shape. Used mostly by fishermen.

corrie: a hollow in a hillside.

cothram: (caw'-rum), justice. Fair play.

creel: a basket.

croft: a small farm, often used for a farm where sheep are raised.

crofter: a farmer.

croodling: huddling and crooning. This is what is called a portmanteau word, very common in Doric or "Braid Scots" dialect.

Cuilleans: (cool'-ans), huge mountains on the Isle of Skye.

daft: wild, crazy.

de'il: devil.

donn: brown.

Each-uisge: (etch-ush'-ka), Water-horse, sea demon. *Each* is a horse, *uisge* is water.

easgadh!: (ess'-geh) (sometimes also spelled *easgaidh*), ready!

eilean: (ay'-llan), a stone or rock: an island.

ell's length: forty inches.

ewes: sheep (female).

fáilte: (fahl-tcha), welcome.

famhair: (favy'-ă-err), monster.

fash one's self: to trouble one's self; to worry or fret.

Glossary

Fiantachd or *Finne:* (fĕh'-ĕnn-tach), the company of Fionn.

fios: (fēēs), wisdom.

forbye: besides, anyway.

gait: way.

gang: go.

gang her ain gait: go her own way.

gavallachan: (găv-al'-la-hăn), a daredevil, a rascal. (From the Gaelic: *diabh-bhalacan:* devil's-boy.)

geal: (gyal), white.

gear: possessions.

gentles: persons of high rank; noblemen and gentlefolk.

ghillies or gillies: outdoor servants.

glee-glashing: clanging of metal on metal.

gloaming: twilight, dusk.

gramalas: (gram'-al-as) (sometimes spelled *greimelas*), strength.

grandam: grandmother.

greeting: weeping.

gruagach: (groo'-ăg-ach), giant or giantess.

grummilie: sour-faced. (From the Gaelic word *grumach:* scowling, sullen.)

hauld your whisht!: Be quiet!

Hogmanay: New Year—a great holiday in Scotland.

hoodie crow: the hooded crow, common in Scotland.

Ian: John.

kist: a chest.

kyne: cattle.

laird: a lord or nobleman.

lave: bathe.

luathas: (lōō'-ăs), swiftness.

Mac-an-Coill'uaine: (Mac'-an-Ka-ŏll'-oo-ann), literally: the Son (*Mac*) of (an) woodland (*Coille*) green (*Uaine*).

MacDeorcha: (MacDyorcha), Son (*Mac*) of Darkness (*Deorcha*). (The modern Gaelic word for darkness is *dorcha.* Deorcha is a very old form still used in the Hebrides.)

machair: the grassy strip that lies above the sea and stretches along the cliffs around the islands.

mark: an old coin of Scotland, once worth about thirteen shillings and four pence ($3.30 American).

mile: (mee'-la), a thousand.

mo graidh: (mo grah'-ēē), my dear. (This is what the Irish "machree" comes from.)

mor: big.

Morag: Sarah.

moran taing: (mō'-ran ta'-eng), thank you. (Literally: many thanks.)

mutch: a cap, usually of white linen with a high gathered crown, and usually, also, with a close-fitting frill on the band.

nattering: nagging.

Och. Ochone: Oh! O-o-o-oh!

omadhaun: (ō'-maw-hawn), a crazy fellow, a fool.

peat hag: a place for cutting peats.

peats: blocks of carbonified moss and vegetable matter burnable when dry, found in bogs.

rascallions: rascals, rogues.

sae: so.

scaur: a mountain peak.

Sean: (Shawn), John (Irish).

Sean Mor Eilean: (Shawn More Ay-llan), legendary founder of the Irish Royal House of Johnstone. (Literally: John of the Big Stone.)

sgeulachdan: (skay-lak'-tan), stories. Frequently means old stories or folk tales.

shieling: (sheeling), cottage. This is not Gaelic, but Braid Scots dialect.

Sidhe: (shee), the Shee or Fairy folk who are as tall as mortals and resemble them in appearance. Sometimes called "The People of Peace."

Glossary

sluagh: (sloo'-ah) (or in some districts: sloo-ag), a lot, a great
   many.

solus: (sawl'-us), light.

spae-wife: a wise woman. A witch.

sporran: a pouch that is hung from the belt.

tarbh-uisge: (tarv'-ush-ka), water-bull, water fairy. *Tarbh* is bull
   and *uisge* is water (fresh water—rivers and burns).

tonn-tunn: (tōnn'-tŭnn), literally: plunge, dive. A word used
   to describe the sound of waves on the shore. A surge and
   retreat of the waves.

trews: trousers.

truagh mo charadh: (troo'-ä-ow mo chah'-rah), sad is my con-
   dition! Pitiful is my case!

weans: toddlers, very small children.

whelk: a sort of shellfish that burrows in the sand of the shore
   and lives on clams.

Whisht!: Hush!

ABOUT THE ARTIST: Born in St. Petersburg, Russia, Vera Bock came to the United States as a child at the onset of the Russian Revolution. At an early age she studied drawing, painting, heraldry, illumination, and wood engraving in Europe. There she also developed an interest in printing and photoengraving which in turn yielded a craftsmanlike concern for a book's appearance as an integrated whole comprising typography and design as well as illustration. Ultimately, Vera Bock the illustrator became Vera Bock the illustrator-designer. The first book she both designed and illustrated, *The Girl Who Would Be Queen*, became one of the American Institute of Graphic Art's Fifty Books of the Year in 1940. Since then her work has appeared in the Fifty Books exhibits and the A.I.G.A. Children's Book Shows as well as at the Metropolitan Museum of Art and the Corcoran, and in the Morgan Library's International Children's Book Show.

ABOUT THE BOOK: The display material is set in Weiss Initials Series I and Weiss Italic; the text is set in linotype Caledonia. The book was printed by offset. Vera Bock, who has been called "the artist of the beautiful macabre," has put into her symbolic interpretations of each of the stories all the feeling of the Western Islands, the sea, the mists, the roughness of the land, and she has evoked the strange and eerie quality of the Gaelic stories. In Miss Bock's own words about the pictures:

> "They're not paintings. They're not drawings.
> There's a little of the one and a little of the other.
> There's brush and pencil, paint and chalk.
> Charcoal dust and eye of newt.
> Water without color, ink without pen,
> and the memory of how fog smells."